MW01093717

HIGH COUNTRY

ALSO BY B.N. RUNDELL

Rindin' Lonesome

Star Dancer

The Christmas Bear

Buckskin Chronicles

McCain Chronicles

Plainsman Western Series

Rocky Mountain Saint Series

Stonecroft Saga

HIGH COUNTRY

A QUEST CHRONICLES NOVEL
BOOK 1

B.N. RUNDELL

WOLFPACK
PUBLISHING
— EST 2013 —

High Country
Paperback Edition
Copyright © 2024 B.N. Rundell

Wolfpack Publishing
1707 E. Diana Street
Tampa, FL 33610

wolfpackpublishing.com

Paperback ISBN 978-1-63977-515-6
eBook ISBN 978-1-63977-514-9
LCCN 2024937250

HIGH COUNTRY

1

REMEMBER

We set sail from Havre de Grace in France, in a ship called St. John, *the second day of May, in the year 1666. Our vessel was equipped with eight and twenty guns, twenty Mariners, and two hundred and twenty passengers; included in this number those whom the company sent as free passengers, as being in their service.*

So BEGAN THE FIRST WORDS OF THE LATEST BOOK TO FALL into the hands of the young man known as Cordell Beckett. An avid reader since he sat as his mother's knee and she taught him the phonics of reading, he reveled in the escapes he enjoyed when he went into the woods, climbed up in his favorite sycamore tree, a massive tree with big branches, and holding his favorite getaway where he could lean back, stretch out his long legs, and escape to other worlds.

The book he held in his lap was *Bucaniers of*

America: Or a True Account of the Most Remarkable Affaults committed of later years upon crafts of The West Indies by the Bucaniers of Jamaica and Tortuga, both English and French. With one hand behind his head to cushion it from the flakes of the mottled bark of the sycamore, and one holding the book on his uplifted lap, his bent legs stationary by his feet on the limb, he was ready to escape into the wild doings of the old buccaneers and pirates of the far seas.

After a glance to the woods around him, ensuring no one had followed, like his younger sister, Marybel, with her long curls of blonde hair and her mischievous ways, he continued reading.

> *Soon after, we came to an anchor under the Cape of Barflor, there to join other seven ships of the fame West India Company, which were to come from Dixp, under the convoy of a man of war, mounted with seven and thirty guns, and two hundred and fifty men. Of these ships two were bound for Senegal, five for the Caribby Islands, and ours for the Island of Tortuga.*

Cord lifted his eyes to the slow-moving clouds that waltzed upon the azure blue sky and let his mind picture the ships at anchor, and himself aboard the *St. John.*

His fantasy lasted just a moment until his reverie was shattered by rifle shots. He frowned, sat up, and looked over the treetops to see a column of smoke rising from where his home sat in the clearing. More gun shots sounded, and Cord was frozen in place, trying to imagine what might be happening. Perhaps his pa was shooting at some varmint, or...but no, there were too many shots, too close together, for it to be one shooter. But who? *Bushwhackers!*

He tucked the book into the knothole reserved for his treasures and made his climb down the big tree. He started at a run back to his home, but as he neared, he remembered the words of his father, *Don't ever go runnin' up on somethin' you don't know! That's a fool's way of getting yourself in a peck o' trouble! Always do a reconnoiter 'fore you go chargin' into trouble!*

The Beckett home was in western Missouri, just south of Harrisonville, the town that had been occupied by Union troops in '61 and became a military post under martial law. That had been lifted just the year before, and the war had been over for almost a year, but because of the isolated location of the Beckett farm, there had always been the threat of trouble from the Kansas Jayhawkers and other renegades that roamed the isolated farmlands.

Cord breathed deep, looking around frantically for some way, some high ground to get a view of what was happening and how best he could intervene if necessary or possible. He spotted another big sycamore and began clawing and scrambling his way up the flaky trunk. Thankfully, this one was not as big as his reading perch, but it was still so big he could not get his arms around the trunk, but he hugged the trunk, used his tough toes of his bare feet, and scooted up to the lowest branch, but still could not see, and climbed higher. He stretched out on a limb, moved a small branch aside and looked into the clearing that held his home. Several mounted riders were moving about, shouting and shooting, all with pistols, but laying in the doorway of their home, outstretched on his belly, was his father, obviously shot, maybe dead.

As he watched, a man came pushing out of the house, stepping over the prone figure of Cord's father and holding what appeared to be the mantle clock from the living room. He was shouting, laughing, and talking to the others, but Cord was too far away to hear and understand what was said. Cord was angered and scared and slid quickly to the ground and started for his home, but now he moved stealthily, keeping under cover and moving through terrain that was his home stomping grounds and no one knew this land better than he did, but his emotions were raging, questions were stomping through his mind, and his heart was trying to beat its way out of his chest.

He dropped into a crouch, moved behind a big oak, went to his belly, and peered around the base of the trunk and watched. The men had ransacked their home, as was evidenced by the many personal belongings he saw scattered about the yard and carried by the Bushwhackers, and he saw no sign of his mother and sister and little brother, Charlie, and the figure of his father had not moved, even though stepped on and over by several of the looters. He looked to the barn where his horse and other animals were sheltered, but they were running free in the field and flames were showing from the back of the barn where the smoke spiraled into the sky. He watched as two men tried to catch his dad's big chestnut horse, but that was a one-man horse that allowed no one, not even Cord, to touch him.

When he looked back to the house, he saw the men tying their booty to their horses and getting mounted, shouting to one another, and they rode from the place, but not before throwing torches through the windows to set the house on fire. As Cord watched them leave, he glanced from them to the house, and started at a run to the back door, knowing he could get inside the back without being seen. He pushed through the door, covered his mouth and nose with his neckerchief in his hand, and moved into the house.

The house had been ransacked and torn apart. Furniture overturned, curtains torn down, windows broken, and the torches were starting to burn the broken furniture and the wooden floor that his father had labored so long and hard to install. He pushed through to the bedroom of his parents, saw the bloodied naked form of his mother spread-eagled on the bed as fire licked at the feather mattress and more. Her blank eyes stared at nothing, and he knew she was dead, then he saw the body of his little sister, her throat slit, her clothing ripped, and her arm torn from its socket and bent backwards. He turned away and looked to the loft, saw an arm hanging over the edge and blood dripping from the fingers, but the smoke boiled up and covered the scene and made Cord choke.

His anger and fear drove him to the back porch where his father's gun cabinet stood. Even though he had been a peaceful preacher in the local church, he had been a man that believed in protecting and providing for his family, and believed a man should be well armed. The box cabinet had been ignored, looking more like a rag bin or something similar, and the lid was still latched. Cord lifted the lid, pushed aside the rags and more, and was relieved to find his father's coach gun shotgun, the Sharps buffalo gun, and his pride, the Remington New Model Army pistol. Cord grabbed them all, ran outside with them and stood them beside the tree, stuffed the pistol in his belt and ran back for the rest of his father's treasures and ammunition for the weapons.

———

A COLD NOSE brought Cord instantly awake. He opened his eyes to the familiar sight of Blue, his faithful mixed blood hound dog. Behind him was the line back grulla stallion that answered to the name of Kwitcher, and Cord shook his head as he sat up, knowing nothing of any danger anywhere about for his faithful friends would have warned him before this. He ran his fingers through his hair, rubbed the sleep from his eyes, and looked around the little clearing where he had made camp the night before. He shook his head as he stood, remembering the dream that was a replay of the actual events of his youth, the time when the Bushwhackers hit his home just across the Missouri border right after the war. But that happened four or five years ago, and try as he might, Cord had been unable to rid his memory of those scenes, vivid as they were, and he was troubled again and again by that memory. Yet when it came, he would try to focus his attention on the raider's faces, endeavoring to imprint their images and voices and anything else that would identify them on his mind.

After he buried his family, Cord had been determined to become the man his folks had always wanted him to be, but to do that Cord believed he had to settle accounts. He stayed with a neighbor, where Joseph McNulty often visited and who would later become a lawman in Lawrence, Kansas, and during his visits to the neighbor's home, helped Cord learn and hone the skills thought necessary for him to settle those accounts. Another neighbor bought the family farm and what little was left of equipment and personal effects. At the encouragement of McNulty, Cord kept his father's Sharps rifle and traded for a Henry repeater now in the scabbard with his saddle. The Remington New model Army in .44 caliber converted for metal cartridges, in a holster on

his hip had replaced the older Remington that was
his father's, but he still had the coach gun shotgun in
a sheath on the pack saddle beside the Sharps, riding
on a pack mule, purchased with the money saved by
his father and stashed under the guns in his gun
cabinet. Now he was starting a search for the renegades who had destroyed his family and he did not
know where that search might take him. McNulty
thought the men that had been with the Jayhawkers
and Red Legs would have left the country and maybe
headed to Colorado and the gold fields that had
drawn so many men in search of riches, but Cord was
not after gold, he was searching for men.

2

KANSAS

CORD SAT BESIDE THE FIRE, WATCHING THE PORK BELLY sizzle in the pan and the coffee begin to perk in the pot and his mind began to drift. He remembered the words of his mentor, McNulty, "You've got more natural talent for handling firearms than any man I've ever seen. Although it's not expected nowadays, but I believe it will be 'fore long, you get that pistol outta that holster and on target faster'n I can blink! Ain't never seen the like, and whatever you wanna shoot, you just up and does it, an' I ain't never seen you miss!"

Cord remembered the times he and McNulty had gone into the woods and set up different objects for targets and the two men would stand beside one another until McNulty would shout the word, "Now! " and they would both grab for their pistols and shoot the target, and invariably Cord would blast all three of his targets before McNulty pulled the trigger the first time.

It was McNulty that gave him his first lead about the Jayhawkers that were rampant in the area during the time when his farm had been attacked and his family massacred. "There's a fella that's got a livery up in Leavenworth, Kansas. He used to be with the Jayhawkers an' others. Now, from what I hear, he's a good man, but he might know what was happenin' 'round here 'bout that time."

As he thought about his quest, he had been driven by a need for vengeance, but his father's words kept coming back to him and even haunting him, "Vengeance is mine, I will repay, saith The Lord. Son, we've known some mighty bad things durin' this war, we've seen some o' the Red Legs an' others come into our church, spyin' on the congregation, tryin' to find those that resist their ways. Some o' the Red Legs from 'round our part of the country, believe in keepin' slaves, and most o' them Bushwhackers from Kansas, well, they say they're abolitionists and are agin' slavery. But their way o' doin' things is often worse than slavery. Now you know we don't believe in slavery. I've taught from God's Word that everybody's the same, no matter the color of their skin, and God loves us all, and that's the way we should be, understand?"

"I do, Pa," answered Cord, and glanced to his best friend, Amos Carpenter, the son of slaves that had been freed and were neighbors of the Becketts. Cord and Amos had spent most of their youth together, and were about the same age, with Cord maybe a little older and definitely bigger. While Cord had a spurt of growth when he became a teen, Amos did not have his until recently. Cord was just thirteen but was already pushing toward the top end of five feet plus and nearing six feet.

Cord chuckled at the memory, poured himself a cup of coffee, and pulled the pan off the fire, and with the tip of his knife, he picked out the bacon and began his breakfast. As he thought about Amos, he shook his head because Amos and his family had been taken by the Jayhawkers under the guise of liberating them and that was the last he had seen of the family. Blue pushed his nose onto Cord's lap, his soulful eyes begging for a tidbit, and Cord chuckled and shared a strip of bacon with his faithful hound dog.

He had been a gangly sixteen-year-old when his farm had been hit, that was in 1865, after the war was over, but Bushwhackers and others under that cover had continued their raids and plundering of homes, farms, villages, and more. Now, Cord was a strapping young man pushing nineteen and standing just over six feet, weighing a little over thirteen stone, or about 185 pounds, broad-shouldered, with dark hair, and a full but well-trimmed beard, narrow hips that held the holster of his pistol cocked at an angle on his left hip, butt forward, giving him easy access even when he wore his ever-present long duster. His tall, crowned wide-brimmed felt hat with a pinch crease and tapered brim that shaded his eyes, added just a touch of mystery about the sun-browned, dark-complected young man.

He had always been a strong man, made so by the hard work on the farm when his father was so often busy with his congregation's needs. But he was also very intelligent, well-read, which was his mother's doing, and quick-witted. He gave all the credit for what he was to his godly parents, but he often fought with his own conscience regarding what he knew was nothing short of a vengeance quest to find the men responsible for his family's murder.

He took a deep breath, stood, and tossed the dregs of the coffee onto the last of the coals of the fire, kicked more dirt on the coals, and turned to saddle his horse and rig up the pack mule. This was the first leg of his journey, he was bound for Leavenworth and a visit with a man formerly known as Captain Tough, whose name was William S. Tough, who operated a livery there and who had been a member of the Kansas Jayhawkers who roamed the Kansas-Missouri border during the war, and maybe was a part of the bunch that raided his farm after the war. McNulty thought he might at least be of help and could identify those who might have been a part of that raid.

The riverbank of the Kansas River was thick with hardwoods—walnut, oak, elms, and Osage Orange, but a trail had been cut through to break into the open at the landing for the Muncie Ferry. Cord had been on the trail for three days and the sun was lowering in the west when he rode up to the ferry and was greeted by the ferryman.

"Howdy friend! Wanna go crost?" he asked.

Cord saw the man was a native and knew the Kaw people and some Wyandotte had been active in building ferries, but that was in years past, and Cord was somewhat surprised to see a native operating the ferry.

"I do. What's the charge?"

"Fifty cents per animal, same for you."

Cord swung down, dug in his pocket for some coin, and paid the man and led the animals aboard. There was a farmer and his wagon and team already aboard, and Cord and animals made a full load. It was an easy crossing, Cord's first experience on a ferry, and he was relieved to feel solid land beneath his feet. He swung aboard his horse and started up the road pointing north. He had talked to the farmer and learned the road would take him northwest and would join the main road that led to Leavenworth. "It'll take you two, three days, dependin' on how fer ya' go each day, an' of course the weather can allus cause problems. But I reckon we ain't in fer no storms soon, so, you'll prob'ly get there 'fore Sunday."

Cord was not a talker, and with a nod to the farmer, he pushed on, wanting to find a campsite before dark, but when the farmer continued, "Say, you got someplace fer the night?"

"Just lookin' for a campsite, mebbe find someplace in the woods, you know."

"My place ain't too fer, an' the missus is a mighty good cook. You're welcome to join us fer supper and you can sleep in the barn. Got a loft wit' some warm hay!" he grinned. "We don' get much comp'ny, an' the missus is allus askin' 'bout folks an' such. She'd be pleased to set a place fer you, if yore of a mind."

"A good home-cooked meal does sound good. All right, I'll stay," answered Cord, motioning to the road, "Lead the way!"

The sun was painting the western sky in shades of bold orange and gold, the colors dripping onto the rolling terrain with farmer's fields and thickets of hardwoods, when the farmer pulled onto a narrow road that split the trees and soon broke into the open, where newly plowed and planted fields showed the hard work of the man. Cord pulled up alongside the wagon as they neared the farmhouse and barn, both showing signs of weathering with logs beginning to show grey and the split wood of the barn showing the same. A hooded well house stood lonely in the yard that had some early blooming flowers of yellow and white, and a screen door opened to show an apron frocked woman shading her eyes to watch the wagon and rider coming near. She smiled, waved, and stepped from the house, wiping her hands on her apron and walking closer as the men neared the barn.

The man stood, looked at Cord and said, "Say, I plum fergot! I'm Sage Warner," he began, grinning, "and this," motioning to the woman that was nearing the wagon, "is muh missus, Suzy!"

Cord nodded to Sage, looked to the woman, and touched his hat brim, "Ma'am. I'm Cordell Beckett, an' I'm afraid your husband has invited me for supper. Hope that's all right?"

She smiled, nodding, "Of course, of course. We're always glad to have company. We seldom get to see a fresh face and hear news of the rest of the world. You're welcome, Cordell."

Cord nodded, swung down, and led the animals into the barn as Sage stripped the team of their harness. After giving both Kwitcher and the mule a quick rubdown and a flake of hay in the mow, Cord stepped to the big door of the barn where Sage stood, thumbs under his galluses, as he surveyed the land before him. When Cord came beside him, he waved his arm and said, "That's muh farm. Cleared and plowed these fields muh own self. That'n," nodding to the west field, "is corn an' beans, an' that'n, is wheat. Hopin' fer a good harvest come fall." He nodded as if putting a period at the end of his sentence and stepped off toward the house. He called over his shoulder, "Missus wants us to wash up!" and headed to the well housing.

3

CONTEMPLATION

WHEN CORD PUSHED BACK FROM THE TABLE AND LAY HIS napkin beside the plate, he smiled at Suzy Warner, "Ma'am, that was a mighty fine meal. I thank you, and you too, Sage. Thanks for the invite, and I best be excusin' myself, I'll be on the trail 'fore first light and I should be checkin' on my animals and turnin' in. Again, I thank you both," he declared as he stood and pushed his chair in and under the table.

"You're very welcome, Mr. Beckett, and if you come back this way, feel free to stop in and have another meal," stated Mrs. Warner, nodding to Cord and to her husband who nodded as well to show his agreement.

"She's right 'bout that, Cord. Anytime you're hereabouts, stop in. We'd be glad to have ya," added Sage.

As Cord exited the door and pulled it closed

behind him, Mrs. Warner looked to her husband, frowning, "He sure don't talk much, does he?"

"But he shore knows how to eat!" chuckled Sage as he stood and began clearing the table to help his wife.

———

THE FIRST LIGHT of early morning had just begun to silhouette the eastern hills when Cord's light stepping grulla stallion started on the roadway heading north. He knew Leavenworth was almost due north and there were several trails that would take him that direction, although there was a primary road that was used by freighters, wagons, and more, he preferred the lesser trails that offered more cover and quieter travel. Although the terrain was rolling hills, it was broken up by farmers making their mark upon the land and clearing the trees and underbrush to be replaced by plowed and planted fields. These Cord tried to pass by unseen.

He was a quiet and contemplative man, seldom needful of companionship or company of any kind, preferring the company of his animals. Both Kwitcher, the grulla stallion, and Blue, the hound dog, seemed to sense that about the man, yet offered themselves as his friends. The mule was a bit more standoffish, preferring his own company to that of others, and only tolerating the company of Kwitcher when necessary.

The trail he followed was set back from the Missouri River yet most times the big muddy was within sight. Come mid-day, Cord came to a little feeder creek, and he spotted a bit of a clearing in the trees near the creek bank and nudged Kwitcher through the trees to the clearing. He stepped down, loosened the girth on his saddle and the pack saddle, and let the animals take some water, and he dropped to the ground in the shade of an Osage Orange tree, watching the animals graze. Blue dropped beside Cord and watched the horses, but searched the trees for anything that might make a tasty snack.

Blue's head came up, his ears perked as much as the long floppies could, and he took off at a run, chasing who knew what. Cord chuckled, believing the dog had spotted a cottontail, because he had learned that to chase any kind of squirrel was a futile endeavor as they could escape up a tree before they could be caught. Cord pulled his hat down over his eyes as he leaned back against the tree, folded his arms across his chest, and let his heavy eyelids drop.

When Kwitcher's head came up, he also stomped a foot that brought Cord instantly awake, but Cord did not move, he watched Kwitcher from under the brim of his hat. The horse nervously side-stepped, his nostrils flared and eyes wide. Cord dropped his right hand to the butt of his pistol under his duster but kept his left arm across his chest, hiding his movement. With another glance to the horse, Cord kept his breathing easy, and watched as Kwitcher stepped back, but with his head still lifted and showing alarm. Cord heard footsteps moving through the leaves, trying to be quiet and he guessed there were at least two.

A whisper broke the stillness, "He ain't movin'. He's sound asleep, hehehe."

"Shhh, you'll wake him 'fore we get what we want. Git'cher gun on him!" came another soft voice as they moved closer.

Cord could see the feet of two men, and let a snort escape as if he was snoring, the sound allowed him to move his head enough to see more and he rolled to the right, drawing and cocking the pistol as he moved.

He growled, "Drop 'em less'n you wanna die!"

His abrupt command startled the intruders, and they stumbled back, bumping into one another as the second man pulled the trigger on his pistol, but the blast sent bullet into the ground as he faltered about. Cord came to his feet, pushed his hat back and glared at the two men, "I don't take kindly to Bushwhackers! Maybe I just oughta kill you here an' now!"

The first man held a big Walker Colt to his side, his thumb on the hammer, but fear in his eyes as he stammered, "We weren't gonna do nuthin' mister, we's just lookin' fer sumpin' to eat! We ain't had nuthin' fer two days!" he whined.

"Drop that pistol!" ordered Cord, glanced to the other man who had fired his pistol, but Cord saw it was a single shot flintlock, and he shook his head, "Drop it!" Both men complied, looking at Cord with wide eyes. The men were dirty, wore ragged clothes, and he could smell them from where he stood. The men dropped their pistols and Cord moved to the side, motioning with his pistol, "Git over there and lay down on your bellies!"

"Why?" whined the first man.

"Do it!" ordered Cord. The men hustled to the tree, dropped to the ground beside it and stretched out on their bellies. "Now, don't be movin'. I'm gonna leave, and if you do as you're told, I'll leave you some vittles!" He heard some mumbles and whispers from the two, but they did not move while Cord tightened the girth on his saddle and on the packsaddle. He swung aboard, turned to look at the men and grabbed the little bag given to him by Mrs. Warner, as he tossed it to the men he said, "There's some corn dodgers in there that'll keep you goin' a while."

Cord nudged Kwitcher to the trail, pulling the lead line of the mule taut, and started across the little creek. When they came from the water, Blue rose from the brush, wagging his tail, and grinning at Cord as he came alongside the horse, keeping pace with the long-legged grulla. Cord thought about the recent happening, knowing it was the way of the country that had been through the bloody and destructive war, and it would take some time before things changed. There would be many former soldiers and other ne'er do well's that would fail to find their way and would seek to do as was done during the war, take what you wanted or needed without any regard to those that would stand to lose. He shook his head remembering the many sermons his father had sounded forth with the need to *love your fellow man, but don't stoop to the ways of evil for any reason!* But isn't that what he was doing on this vengeance quest trying to find those who murdered his family and plundered their farm?

He shook his head, trying to clear his mind of the images of his family's destruction and the heart break pain in his chest returned as a reminder of the need for what he preferred to call justice. He believed that would be the only way he would find peace in his heart and mind and be able to get on with his life, whatever or wherever that may lead.

His mind turned to his father, remembering some of the things he learned. His father had fought with the British during the Battle of Pinjarra and had received an officer's commission. He also fought with the Ottoman Empire as an officer during the revolt in Tripolitania. Although his father would never talk about his war-time exploits, he shared with Cord the many ways of fighting he learned. What had suited Cord the best was the hand-to-hand combat or what would become known as martial arts. What he learned from his father was a unique blend of Muay Thai and capoeira with elements of jiu-jitsu. But Cord had developed his own style using moves from all those taught by his father, for his father always said, "You have to use what is natural and comfortable for you, not what works for others. Sometime you may have to defend your life, or the lives of others and you won't have a weapon other than your own body."

But as he remembered, he would always wrestle with the conflict of fighting and loving, but it was never a conflict in his father's mind and life, even though the words that seemed to ring the loudest in Cord's memory were the words of his father and the Bible that said in John 15:12 *This is my commandment, that ye love one another, as I have loved you. Greater love hath no man than this, that a man lay down his life for his friends.* And that memory always brought back his father's explanation, "You see son, love is self-sacrifice. It's not some fuzzy feeling about someone special, like when you love your family or your wife or...God showed it best in John 3:16 *For God so loved the world, that he gave...* That's self-sacrifice, that's love."

Cord spoke out loud as if his father was beside him, "But Pa, they murdered our family! They've got to pay for that! You can't expect me to love them! Can you?" He had startled himself with his outburst and Kwitcher stopped and turned his head to look at him, and Blue jumped up and put his paws on Cord's leg, both animals surprised at his speaking aloud. Cord chuckled, reached down to rub behind Blue's ears, and leaned forward to stroke Kwitcher's neck, talking to them both and glancing to the mule who stood still, chewing on a mouthful of grass, concerned about nothing but his own hunger. Cord had been harboring these thoughts of vengeance for most of three years; it was his purpose for almost everything he had done—learning to fight, shoot, hunt, and more, and what he had worked for, destined for, was now in motion.

Cord took a deep breath, shook his head at his repeated thoughts, and nudged the grulla into a walk to continue on their trek northward and what he considered to be his appointment with destiny.

4

LEAVENWORTH

WHEN HE CRESTED THE SLIGHT HILL AND LOOKED BELOW, he was astounded at the sight before him. Houses, buildings, businesses, streets, and more galore. He had never seen the like and he reined up, leaned on the pommel of his saddle, and pushed his hat back as he took in the wonder of it all. Before him lay the oldest city in the state of Kansas, Leavenworth. Block upon block of buildings of all shapes, sizes, and construction, while below it all the Missouri River held riverboats, some docked, others moored, and several upon the water, their paddlewheels churning the muddy waters while their smokestacks belched black smoke.

He had read about such places that existed over in Europe or back east in the states and knew the nation was growing and people were moving west, but...he shook his head in wonder and nudged Kwitcher forward, pulling the lead line taut because the mule had stopped and stared and apparently did not like the smell of things, and only begrudgingly followed. The road that Cord followed had stayed near the west bank of the Missouri, and now pointed into town where he saw a two-story building with a sign that said Miller Bros. Tannery and he recognized the stench of such. He rode past, saw a small sign that indicated he was at the corner of Elm and Second Streets, and Elm Street was an east/west street, and a short distance to Cord's right, it joined another that was closer to the waterfront. He had been told that Tough's Livery was near the waterfront, so he nudged his mount that direction, turned north at the end of Elm on Main Street and within six blocks, all of which held buildings on the west side, but nothing but sloping land down to the water on the east, he came to a long building with corrals and more that told Cord he had found the livery.

He kneed Kwitcher to the big double doors at the front of the building where he heard the clang of hammer on anvil that was the giveaway of a blacksmith. He stepped down, looked into the big doors to see a man with a leather apron standing near a forge with tongs holding a horseshoe and his other hand with a hammer. He waited till the man turned to face him and he nodded, watching the man work with the hot iron and when he finished and looked up, Cord said, "Howdy! Got room for muh horse an' mule?"

"I do." He motioned to the stalls behind him,

"Pick out a couple, put 'em away. There's hay in the stack yonder, so throw 'em a flake or two and there's water in the trough and a place for water in the stall. You can carry it if'n you like, or just let 'em get water first."

Cord nodded and set about stripping the animals and stashing his gear in the tack room. He walked back to the front of the building where the smithy had put away his tools and was sitting in a ladder-back rocker at the doorway, looking at the traffic on the river. Cord approached the man and asked, "You the owner, Bill Tough?"

"I am. And you?"

Cord extended his hand, "I'm Cordell Beckett, from down country, over the line in Missouri. Headin' west."

"You look like a man that's got questions. What can I help you with, Cordell Beckett from down country?"

Cord grinned, dropped his eyes, and looked back up at Tough, "You know a man named McNulty?"

Tough frowned, "McNulty, McNulty, sounds familiar. Reckon I knowed a couple McNulty's in the war."

"Joseph McNulty, young man, family out west o' here, I think he said it was Rooks County."

"Don't remember him, what's he got to do with you'n me?"

"He said you're a good man and had some experience with the Jayhawkers an' Red Legs," began Cord, but paused when Tough came to his feet from the rocker, and stepped back with a guarded expression, but he continued, "The reason I ask, I was lookin' for information on a raid that took place after the war. McNulty said you might know some o' the fellas that were a part of it. It was down south of Independence, and they went through Butler, Harrisonville, Clinton, and Osceola—this was after the war."

Tough backed up another step, reached for his hammer that lay on the bench and growled at Cord, "You implying I was part o' that?"

Cord shook his head, "No, not at all. Matter of fact, McNulty swore that you would not have been a part. He said you were too good a man to stoop to such doin's."

Tough visibly relaxed, and looked at Cord, "So, what are you plannin' to do?"

"I'm just lookin' for information, maybe some names."

"And if you get names, then what?"

"Mr. Tough, those men murdered my father, despoiled my mother, killed my sister and brother, and burnt our family's home down around 'em. I don't rightly know what I'll do when I find any of 'em, *if* I do, but I'm compelled to try to find them. My father was a preacher that always preached forgiveness and such, but before I can do that, I need to find them."

Tough frowned, sighed, put the hammer down and looked at Cord, "You had supper yet?"

"No sir. Been travelin' for a few days."

Tough looked at Cord, "If that happened right after the war, that's been two, three years, why look now?"

"I wasn't full growed when I was up in the tree watchin' 'em. And I had some growin' and learnin' to do. Now I'm ready to find 'em, and..." he shrugged.

Tough turned, looked to the waterfront, then back to Cord, "Let's go get somethin' to eat and we'll talk. There's a little café I go to quite often, good food, good folks, you'll like it."

Cord nodded, motioned to Bill, "Lead the way, I'm so hungry my stomach thinks muh throat's been cut!"

———

It was a cozy little place on the corner of Cherokee and Main, just one block back from the waterfront. A clapboard building, one story, big windows, and a squeaky sign that declared it to be Ma's Place. When Bill pushed through the door, he was greeted by a matronly woman standing behind a counter, adorned with a broad smile that split her face under a red bulbous nose. "Hi there, Bill! Brought me 'nother eater, huh?"

"I did, Ma. What's the special?"

"Got some fried catfish! Fresh today! Chitlin's, coffee, greens an' more. Ain't gonna tell ya what the 'more' is, gotta guess!" she cackled and laughed as she turned to the kitchen, calling over her shoulder, "Two of 'em, comin' up!"

Bill chuckled as he sat down at a table, Cord did as well and looked at Bill, "Chitlins?"

With a broad grin, he asked, "Never had chitlins? You're in for a treat—deep fried, spicy...Ma's from New Orleans and it's a southern thing."

Cord looked around and was surprised to see a table with four uniformed soldiers, all of them colored. One man had his back to Cord but wore sergeant's stripes and was busy with his food, as were the others. It was not a common thing to see coloreds sitting with whites in a restaurant, but he knew that this was Kansas and Kansas had been a free state and many of the coloreds from slave states had come across the Missouri to make their homes here. He turned back to Bill.

"So, what can you tell me?"

"I knew a lot of the men that rode with the Jayhawkers and Red Legs, did myself for a while. But I got away from it when things started getting out of hand. I went to the Buckskin Scouts under General Blunt as part of the Army of the Frontier. There were several men in the scouts that had also been with the Red Legs. I remained friends with several of the men and some others left the Red Legs to work with us, like Bill Cody and others. Even after I left 'em, I kept my ear to the ground, so to speak, and heard a lot of reports about some of 'em. There were good men, and they also attracted more than their share of bad ones."

"Ever run into Quantrill?"

Bill frowned, "Yeah, but he wasn't a Red Leg, he was in the war. That's where I ran into him. His bunch attacked a column I was scoutin' for and he done some damage that day."

The men leaned back as Ma came to pour the coffee. She stood stoically to the side, frowned and asked, "You two don't look hungry 'nuff for what I'm 'bout to bring!" she covered her mouth as she giggled lightly.

"Now Ma! You know better'n that! Have you ever brought me a plate that I didn't clean up?" retorted a grinning Bill.

"Oh, reckon not, but what about him?" she asked, motioning to Cord.

"Well, just you bring the plate and let me do my best, will you?" chuckled Cord.

Ma turned away, giggling as she started to the kitchen, but the sergeant at the table of colored soldiers turned and looked at the two talkers. He frowned, and asked, "Your name Cordell?"

Cord frowned, "That's my name, Cordell Beckett. Who's askin'? " he answered, speaking slowly, looking at the man and frowning.

A big grin split the man's face and he jumped to

his feet and came to the table, extending his hand, "Don't you know me? I'm Amos Carpenter! We grew up together! "

Cord came to his feet and the two men gave one another a bear hug and laughed all the while, slapping one another on the back as they did. When they pulled apart, Cord said, "So, you're in the Army now! If that don't beat all!"

"Yesssir! And that ain't all! The comp'ny commander wants me to go to West Point, become an officer!"

Cord chuckled, looked at his friend, shook his head and laughed. "It is so good to see you, Amos. I don't know how many times I wondered whatever happened to you, but try as I might, I couldn't find out anything!"

"Say, how's your folks doin'? They all right?"

Cord sat down, motioned for Amos to sit as well, and said, "No, there was a band of outlaws hit our place after the war, claimed to be Red Legs, but I dunno. Killed ever'body." Cord dropped his eyes, breathed deep. Looked at Bill, back to his friend, "Amos, this here is Bill Tough, he owns the livery back yonder. Bill, this is Amos Carpenter, my neighbor and friend growin' up."

Amos shook hands with Bill, slapped Cord on the back, "I've gotta go, get the men back to the fort. If you can, stop by 'fore you leave. They can tell you at the gate where to find me!"

"I'll do that!" declared Cord, and turned back to

the table as Ma was setting the plates and more on the table, humming all the while. The food smelled delicious and all of Cord's attention was captured by the chitlin's, greens, and catfish with a plate of hot cornmeal muffins sitting in the center.

5

TRAIL

Cord lay on his back, one hand behind his head as he held the scrap of paper with the names. He had rolled out his blankets in the hay loft of the livery, and with the loft door open, the moonlight rode a long beam into the loft, offering ample light to read. He mumbled the names aloud, *Charles "Doc" Jennison, "Red" Clark, Jim Lane*—those were the leaders, *Newt Morrison, Jack Hays, James Flood, Charles "one-eyed" Blunt, Jerry Malcolm, Dave Poole.* He remembered what Tough said, "I don't know who was on the raid, but I know those last six men rode together, and Doc and Red mighta been leadin' 'em, but more'n likely it was Jim Lane. I suggest you just nose around an' listen. They might still be together, but I doubt it cuz they were a hard bunch and mighta done split up and gone their separate ways. Last I heard, which was nothing but rumor, some of 'em headed west to the gold fields, not that they were lookin' to work and dig their own gold, they just figgered it might be an easy place to 'lift some pokes' from some of the gold hunters."

Cord was thinking about what Tough had said about the men and their way of 'hunting' for their plunder. "The easiest way to go west is on the train, but you won't find out anything about 'em doin' that, cuz they'd never ride the rails, they'd stick to the trails, knowing they would pass travelers, farms, settlers and the like that they'd figger would be easy pickin's. So, if'n I was you, I'd take the trail that's most traveled, the old Santa Fe Trail, cuz there'll be freighters, settlers, and more and you might pick up some news about 'em, leastways, that's what I'd do if I was huntin' 'em."

Before they left Ma's Place, Amos Carpenter had returned, and the two old friends spent some time together after Tough left to go home to his wife and family. Amos explained, "I din't know it afore, but when I got back to the fort, the captain told me I was leavin' in the mornin' to take a squad of replacements to the 10th out to Fort Hays. Be leavin' at first light, so...reckon we won't be seein' one another for some time, if ever."

"You never know, Amos. You're goin' west to Fort Hays, I'm goin' west too, just takin' a different way, headin' a little south, catchin' the Santa Fe Trail, maybe get a job with one of the freighters or sumpin'. Mebbe we'll meet up sometime down the road a spell."

"You think you'll find any them fellas yore lookin' fer?"

"Dunno, all I can do is try."

"Watcha gonna do if'n you find 'em?"

Cord dropped his eyes, looked at his hands, and mumbled, "That's a tough question. I just don't know. Sometimes I get to rememberin' and I get all fired up and if I was to find 'em I'd wanna do to them what they done to muh family." He paused, looked up at Amos, "Then other times the words of muh pa go runnin' through my mind and all I hear is 'You hafta forgive one another, no matter what's been done. You can't change the past, it'd be like tryin' to make a river run upstream, you just can't do it. When you forgive you take a load off'n your heart and mind."

"Ummhmm, that's sounds like my folks, an' muh pa used to quote from the Bible, just like yore pa used to."

"Yup. But doin' that ain't easy, especially when the image of what they done comes back most ever' night," growled Cord. They had been walking along the riverbank, watching the moonlight dance on the waves of the slow-moving big muddy river, while a late arriving sternwheeler pushed against the current and pointed its bow to the wharf. They turned back to the livery and Amos stopped, looked at his friend, extended his hand, "Cord, I hope and pray the best for you and that you get those demons stilled within you. We're both still young and have a lotta life before us, so, let's just make a pact, here and now, to pray for one another and that the best things will come our way, whatsay?"

Cord accepted his hand, let a slow grin split his face, and nodded, "I'm all for that, Amos. And I'll be prayin' 'bout you goin' to West Point." He shook his head, thinking about his friend doing what no other colored man had done, to go to the military academy and come out an officer. "That will be somethin', yessir."

They shook hands, gave one another a bear hug and a slap on the back, stepped back, and looked at one another and as Amos turned away, Cord dropped his eyes and breathed deep as he started back to the livery, his mind already turning to his mission, whether it would be one of vengeance or forgiveness.

Cord rolled over to his side, pulled the blanket over his shoulder and was soon asleep, but his slumber was stirred by the memories and recurring dreams, and the sound of creaking hinges as the big door was opened, brought him instantly awake. He looked about, knew that Blue was sleeping in Kwitcher's stall next to the mule, but there were other horses in the stalls and more in the corral. Cord slowly sat up, looking about and heard the sounds of two men approaching the stalls as one spoke softly and asked the other, "Where's the saddles?"

"In the tack room, yonder. Let's pick out the horses we want first, then we can lead 'em to the tack room and not hafta carry the gear!" declared the second man.

Cord pulled his pistol from the holster that lay beside his rolled-up blanket he used as a pillow, and carefully and quietly moved to the edge of the loft where he could look down into the rest of the livery barn. He was over the stalls, and he saw the dark shadows of two men moving along the alleyway between the two rows of stalls. It was obvious they were looking over the stock, and not searching for their own, when the first man said, "I want that black'un. He looks good."

"I'll take that grulla there," replied the second man. Cord grinned and chuckled to himself; *This is gonna be good!* He knew Kwitcher was a one-man horse and would not allow any other man to touch or ride him and Blue was in the stall with him. Cord moved closer to the edge, bellied down so he could see over the edge without exposing too much of himself and as the first man opened the stall with the black, Cord broke the silence of the night when he cocked the hammer on his pistol. Both men froze in their tracks, ducking down behind the poles of the stalls and looking around.

"You hear that?" whispered the first man in the stall with the black.

"Yeah," answered the second, just as Kwitcher hunched his back and let loose with both rear hooves, driving the man through the boards of the stall gate, breaking the gate and much of the man.

The crash and rattle of the man through the gate and the broken boards caused the first man to shout, "What's happenin'?"

Cord answered with a chuckle, "Your friend just paid the price of horse stealin' and you're about to!"

The man lifted his eyes to the dark loft, saw nothing but black and looked to the big door standing open and started to move, but Cord's voice stopped him with, "Don't do it!" He chuckled, "You're forgettin' your partner! Now drag his worthless tail outta here 'fore I shoot you just for general principles!"

His partner was writhing on the pile of broken boards, moaning and whimpering. The second man went to him, looked up at the loft, "I cain't carry him!" he whined.

"Didn't ask you to, *drag* him outta here 'fore I shoot the both of you, or come down there and put a rope around your neck an' hang you from the rafters!"

The man hurriedly grabbed one arm of his downed partner and began dragging him, much to the complaining and moaning of his partner, but within a few moments of Cord chuckling and shaking his head, the two made it out of the door and into the darkness of the night. Cord went back to his blankets, holstered his pistol and looked out the loft door. The moon was lowering in the west and the day was coming. He rolled his blankets, jammed his feet into his boots, strapped on his holster, put on his hat and duster, and went to the ladder to drop into the livery and begin saddling his horse.

He finished gearing up his animals, started to lead them from the stall area, and saw someone approaching the open door left ajar by the would-be horse thieves. The shadow told Cord it was Bill Tough, the smithy, and he kept moving. He heard Bill mumble, "Now how'd this door get open? I know I latched it tight."

Cord answered from the darkness, "You had a couple fellas wanted to get some horses, but they forgot they didn't have any horses. Me'n Kwitcher here kinda discouraged 'em. You might hafta repair one o' the gates back yonder. Kwitcher kicked one of 'em through the gate."

Cord came into the dim light of early morning to see the confused expression on Bill's face and chuckled, "I wasn't gonna get up this early, but..." he shrugged, grinning. He dug in his pocket and brought out a couple coins, held them out to Bill, "Here's what I owe ya."

"If you stopped a couple horse thieves, I reckon I owe you," answered a frowning Bill Tough.

Cord chuckled, "Well, let's just say they didn't appreciate me ruinin' their plans, but they ruined my sleep, so, guess we're even."

"You know who they were?"

Cord chuckled, "I only know three people in this town, my friend Amos, you, and Ma. Now it wasn't you or Amos, and I'm pretty sure Ma was busy fixin' breakfast, so...nope, don't know who they were," he grinned as he stepped aboard Kwitcher.

"How 'bout I buy you breakfast, then?" asked Bill, looking up at Cord.

"Thanks, but I better get on the trail. Got a long ways to go and sun's comin' up, so..." he shrugged, nodded, and kneed Kwitcher from the livery. He paused, leaned on the pommel, and turned back to look at Bill, "How far to Lawrence?"

"Oh, you can make it in a long day, or you could stop around Tonge-Noxie, go on the next day, short day. Just head out thataway; you'll come to a road called the Tonge-Noxie road, it bears southwest. You'll cross a couple creeks, the second one in the flats is just 'fore you get to the town. Livery there's owned by a friend, Shorty Williams. Tell him I sent'chu an' he'll put you up for the night."

"Any advice for Lawrence?"

"Yeah, keep your mouth shut, your eyes open, and git in an' get out!"

Cord grinned, shook his head, and started away with a wave over his shoulder to Bill.

6

TONGE-NOXIE

THERE WAS NOTHING MEMORABLE ABOUT THE RIDE FROM Leavenworth other than it was an enjoyable time of solitude and reflection for Cord. The terrain was repetitive, creeks with lots of trees—maple, cotton-wood, ash, oak, hackberry, and sycamore. Open fields planted by the farmers, clearings that held white-tail deer, and tall grass and fresh blooming spring flowers, but few travelers, and those he encountered were less than friendly, of course it didn't help that Cord kept to the trees and out of sight most of the time. But the rolling hills and easy traveling terrain kept Cord's interest; it was a fresh and growing country, with new greenery erasing the scars of the recent war and offering hope and promise for the future.

He was breaking from the trees when he saw movement in the clearing and quickly reined up. A white-tail doe stood at the far end of the clearing, and just behind and beside her were a pair of spotted fawns. The mother stepped in front of the fawns, protecting them from the view of the unwelcome intruder and Cord sat, unmoving and watching, a broad smile splitting his face as he enjoyed the sight of new life, innocent yet guarded. The doe nudged her offspring into the trees and the trio quickly disappeared and Cord returned to the open road, knowing he was nearing the town of Tonge-Noxie. He stopped at the creek that meandered through the wide-open flats, shouldered close by the common cottonwoods, hackberry, and elms, with ample willows for company. He let Kwitcher have a good drink, dipped his cupped hand in the water, and quenched his thirst, always watching the surroundings as he sipped the cool water from his palm.

He knew it was Sunday, having passed the Congregational Church on his way out of town early this morning and saw a few buggy teams already being put away in the shed behind the church, and he expected to see the same scene in Lawrence. As he stood beside Kwitcher, his hand on the grulla's mane, he saw a buggy coming from town and heading to the road that led to a farmhouse and barn set back near the trees. The couple in front and some youngun's in the back were laughing and talking, and most likely looking forward to getting home, the sun was lowering in the west and daylight was needed to finish the farm chores. He grinned, remembering the many times his family had done the same thing every Lord's day. He watched as they turned from the road to their roadway that would take them home. Cord waited until they pulled up at the house before he mounted up and took to the road.

As he started into town, he took note of the freshness of the town, most buildings showed little sign of aging and wear, although the Halstead and Halstead Mercantile appeared to be older than most and the clapboard was grey with sun aging. There were people walking about, a few horses at the hitchrails, mostly in front of the Ace's High saloon. He passed a bank building, a hotel, saw a couple of cafés that sat opposite one another, and at the edge of town was the railroad station, the livery, and the beginnings of a log building that already had a sign designating it as a school. Set back behind the hotel, was a new-looking building with a bell tower and a cross on top, marking the town's newer church building.

The livery was off the main road on to the south side with the creek running behind it, and he nudged Kwitcher to the big open door. He grinned, thinking that the livery kept longer hours than the church house or the saloon. As he came to the door, he saw a man sitting in a ladder-back chair that leaned back on two legs against the wide boards of the exterior. A corn-cob pipe let a curl of smoke rise above the wrinkled face of the man who watched Cord with a critical eye as he neared.

"What'cha need, stranger?"

Cord reined up, leaned on the pommel, "A friend of yours up to Leavenworth, told me you'd put up muh animals and me, if'n I asked you real nice. Bill Tough was his name."

At the familiar name, the smithy grinned, dropped his chair to all four legs, and slowly rose, pulling the loose strap of his coveralls over his bare shoulder, and answered, "Step down. I reckon I got a spare stall fer your animals, don't know 'bout'chu though! You look a little salty!" he chuckled and grinned as he said it.

As the man stood and motioned to the interior of the livery, it was obvious where he got his nickname of Shorty, standing well shy of five feet, but with a girth that showed few limits, the man seemed to waddle into the darker interior of the building. He motioned to a couple empty stalls, added, "There's hay up in the loft, you can throw down some to your animals. Fix yo'self a bed up there while you're at it, if'n you wanna. There's water in the troughs, if'n you need more, you'll hafta carry it!"

Cord led his horses into the stalls, climbed into the loft and forked down some hay. He came down the ladder to get his gear, looked at the man, "Kinda quiet in town, that cuz it's Sunday?"

"Nope, it's just early. Things'll liven up a mite later. There's been kinda ree-union of some fellers from the war, an' they's trouble. Might be smart to stay away from there, less'n you wanna be weighted down with a mite o' lead, hehehehe," cackled the smithy, chewing on the stub of his pipe. "I could tell right off you weren't from these parts. Where'bout you hail from?"

"Oh, here'n there. Muh pa was a preacher, so we never settled anywhere fer too long. 'Fore I come along, he'n Ma started out some'ere 'round Phillydelphia, but I don' remember that."

"Where ya' headed?" asked Shorty, cocking up one eyebrow to show his skepticism and suspicion.

"Oh, west, I reckon. Hear tell they's still findin' gold out in the Rocky Mountains some'eres. Had many gold hunters from here go there?"

"There was a handful o' ne'er do wells from here'bouts that heard that siren call a while back. Reckon there was oh, mebbe eight or ten of 'em, give or take. I was glad to see'm go, they was trouble 'round here, allus gettin' in fights an' such. Kilt one man, a good 'un, family man, right 'fore they lit out. They said they was goin' fer gold, but if'n I know folks, them fellers are too lazy to dig for anything, even gold, less'n they's diggin' it from a dead man's pockets!"

Shorty spit a wad from his mouth, wiped his chin, and relit his pipe. Cord grinned and shook his head at the thought of chewing tobacco at the same time as smoking a pipe. He considered them both nasty habits and had tried chewing one time, swallowed some of the juice and was sicker'n a hound dog that caught a skunk, even turned green around the gills. He laughed at the memory and finished stowing his gear at the front of the stall, and tossed his bedroll and saddlebags into a pile, lay his weapons on top and with a nod to the smithy, "Think I'll go for a walk down by the creek, after I put muh gear in the loft."

"Ain't nobody gonna bother it, I sleep in muh room right yonder," he said, pointing to a room behind the forge that had a door standing open and the last of the daylight bending into the single window.

"Any fish in the creek?" asked Cord.

"Nuttin' but catfish, and they's hard to get less'n you go noodlin'."

"I've done that before, but I think I might wait till mornin' to have a good meal at a café 'fore I hit the trail again. Tired of muh own cookin'. Which one would you recommend?"

"I usually eat at the BonTon, it's got a fancy name but it ain't all that much. But the food's always good, an' her breakfast is the best! She makes flapjacks that're lighter'n a feather and has a syrup that she made from some local blackberries, ummmm! Makes me wanna eat breakfast three times a day!" He laughed, and after a short pause with a slow grin, he continued, "She's right nice to look at too, kinda plump, but comfy, if'n you know what I mean, hehe-hehe. Been thinkin' 'bout askin' her to marry me, but she stands head'n shoulders taller'n me an' a woman should look up to her man," he shook his head, his face losin' its smile.

―――――

AND BREAKFAST WAS INDEED A DELIGHT, and the woman, Adelaide, showed herself to be quite friendly with Shorty, and paid little attention to Cord until he asked about the men that went to the mountains to look for gold. "You missin' any of those gold hunters that went to the Rockies? Surely they spent time in here, good as your cookin' is, I reckon every single man spent quite a bit of time in here."

"Oh that bunch? Ever'body was happy to see 'em go! They're the last of the Red Legs that caused so much trouble and they couldn't get it into their heads the war was over! Humph!" she declared as she refilled their cups with steaming coffee. She looked from Shorty to Cord and frowned, "I hope you know that pokin' a bear with a willow stick is safer'n sassin' a woman with a pot o' hot coffee!" she said as she lifted the pot in a threatening manner and with one hand on her hip and her eyes glaring at Cord. "Keep it up an' you ain't gettin' anymore o' them flapjacks!"

Cord shrugged his shoulders, lifted his eyebrows, and held both hands out, palms up and said, "Sorry ma'am, din't mean nuthin'. I apologize an' please bring us some more o' them delicious flapjacks! Please?"

She turned to Shorty, winked, and asked, "You want some more, Sunshine?"

"You know better'n to ask that question, Addy," drawled a smiling Shorty, looking up at his favorite woman. She smiled back, nodded, and trotted off to the kitchen to swap the coffee pot for some flapjacks.

7

LAWRENCE

THE SUN WAS HIGH OVERHEAD IN THE EARLY AFTERNOON AS Cord left the main road to follow what appeared to be a well-used trail that took to the trees and away from the scattered bits of farmland. Within a few moments he broke from the trees on the northeast bank of the Kaw river and recognized this as a shallow water crossing. He stepped down, led the animals to the water and had a better look at the free-flowing river. He shaded his eyes and looked across the wide body of water that stretched about two hundred yards of easy water and it appeared to be reasonably shallow.

After the animals had their drink, he swung back aboard the grulla and nudged him into the water. The big stallion was confident in his strides, but picked his steps carefully as the current pushed against his long legs. With a few steps, they were in water that almost reached the bottom of Cord's stirrups, but the grulla kept his stride, followed closely by the mule. The dog, Blue, swam beside and downstream of the grulla, his ears floating to the side as he paddled across the river. When they climbed from the water, Cord stepped down, let the animals have a halfhearted roll, and he climbed back aboard and started to the town.

There had been a few buildings on the north side, but the town lay on the southwest side of the river and was well spread out. Cord knew this was the beginning of his search. He had asked enough questions, and had the beginning of what he would need, but from here on out, he was determined to listen and learn, but not make others suspicious or even aware of his presence.

His pa had often told him, "Boy, God gave you two ears an' only one mouth! That oughta tell ya' somethin'! And I ain't never heered of anyone learnin' anything by talkin'!" Cord chuckled at the memory, one of many memories of his father and family that he harbored and often recalled to keep the memory of his family alive.

As he neared the town, he passed a large windmill that reminded him of the stories his father told about the time he was in Europe. Sitting high on a hill that overlooked the town was a two-story brick building with a tower atop that he would later learn was the first building of the University of Kansas. He was surprised to see so many three and four-storied brick buildings. The first one he passed was a hotel with a squeaky sign hanging out that said Eldridge House. There were other hotels, several businesses with one larger building holding the Mercantile Store, and all the businesses seemed to be interspersed with saloons and dance halls.

He had no plans of staying in Lawrence, knowing this had been the seat of the Free Staters and had been sacked and looted and mostly destroyed by Quantrill near the end of the war, but it had been rebuilt and little evidence remained of that raid. He knew he had to be careful and do his best to be as obscure as possible, but he hoped to learn something about the renegade Red Legs that had hit his home. He reined up outside the Oriental Saloon, slapped the reins around the hitchrail, and stepped up to the boardwalk, pushed into the dark interior and stood to the side, letting his eyes become accustomed to the dim light.

Several tables held a few patrons, four or five stood at the bar, and two women were circulating hustling drinks. A few looked at Cord but paid him no mind as he walked to the end of the bar and leaned both forearms on the counter. The bartender approached, his apron covered front hiding a protruding belly, and his thin hair waxed down atop his dome, a handlebar moustache draped over his mouth, but his dark eyes were piercing and obviously sizing up the newcomer. "What'll it be?" he growled.

"Beer," answered Cord, glancing around the interior.

He stood relaxed, his loose duster showing signs of travel with dust in the creases, his hat showed dust on the brim and crown, but with the brim turned down and the dark whiskers, it was hard for anyone to get a good look at the man. Although Cord was young in years, he was older in experience and size. He had the full face of whiskers to add to his obvious years, and his deep voice spoke of both experience and age. When the bartender sat the foam topped mug before him, Cord placed a dollar coin on the bar, and reached for the mug. He took a long draught, and stood quietly, appearing to be deep in thought, offering no opening for conversation.

The bartender, busy wiping off the counter, made his way toward Cord, lay the coins in change before him, and asked, "You new 'round here?"

Cord glanced up at the man, shook his head, and took another sip and set the mug down. He looked at the man from under the brim but stood silently.

"Passin' through?" asked the barman.

Cord nodded, mumbled, "Ummhmm."

The bartender leaned on his side of the bar near Cord, "If you're lookin' for work, I had a man in this mornin' said he was with a freighter bunch that's camped 'tween here'n the trail, just south of town. He said they're wantin' to find some muleskinners, helpers, and a hunter."

Cord was nursing the beer, taking his time, and he nodded to the barman, "Thanks."

The barman moved away, realizing the visitor

was not very talkative and went to a group of three at the far end of the bar. It was obvious he was talking about Cord as the three men turned to look at him, then back to the barman. As he lifted the mug again, he heard conversation from the table behind him, "Yeah, they called themselves Border Ruffians, pretended to be Red Legs, but they was nothin' but thugs and troublemakers. One of 'em, Dave Poole, he's been around these parts for a long time. I remember his folks, but he tried to say they were friends of Jim Lane an' I know better'n that, Jim wouldn't had anything to do with the likes of them. I'm glad the whole bunch left; things have been kinda peaceable since."

Another of the three leaned forward and asked, "Where'd they go, you know?"

"Dunno for sure, but someone said they was talkin' 'bout tryin' fer gold out Colorado way."

The third man chimed in, "Pshaw! Ain't a one of 'em willin' to use a pick an' shovel! If it ain't got a trigger on it, they ain't touchin' it!"

As Cord finished off his drink, he sat the mug down, nodded to the bartender and turned to leave, but he paused as the three men, all older with a touch of grey in their head, leastways two of them had grey, the third didn't have enough hair to show color. They were typical of the bar hoppers in any town. Cord let them leave, then casually walked out of the bar to the hitchrail and mounted Kwitcher and started down the street. He looked at each building as he passed, saw another likely looking tavern, and reined up in front, tethered the animals, ordered Blue to stay with Kwitcher, and walked into the bar.

The scene was similar to that he'd just left. The interior was brightly lit with chandeliers, more women circulated, and the clientele appeared to be a little better dressed and talkative. Most tables had card players with a house dealer, made obvious by his long sleeves held up with garters and the round wooden poker chip holder before them. The noise level was higher, but there was room near the end of the bar and Cord made his way that direction. As he looked around, he knew he was conspicuous with his manner of dress, the long duster hanging from his shoulders and drooping to his boot tops, but he did not lock eyes with anyone, and stood at the bar until the bartender asked, "What'chu drinkin'?"

"Beer," answered Cord with a low voice. His eyes were barely visible under the brim of his hat, and the barman frowned, turned away to draw the beer, and soon returned. Cord put a quarter on the counter and reached for the mug as the barman took the coin. Cord leaned on the bar, slowly nursing the beer, listening. This was a more talkative bunch, even the card players did more than shuffle and hold their cards, often spinning yarns as they played.

His attention turned to a conversation from a table of five men that were drinking and talking, when one man said, "Yeah, he tried to say he rode with Doc Jennison, but I know better. I was with Doc an' I never saw the likes of him!"

"Who you talkin' 'bout, George?" asked one, frowning and leaning forward.

"Oh that whippersnapper, I think his name was Newt somethin' or other. He was allus drinkin', cussin', chasin' the women, never did amount to much."

"Didn't he leave with that bunch that hung around the Three Deuces?"

"I think so, ain't seen 'em in a good long while, which makes things a bit more peaceable," grumbled the first speaker.

"If'n I 'member right, that bunch would come'n go ever few months, but it's been a good while since we seen any of 'em."

"Good riddance, I say. One of 'em started work fer me, didn't do nuthin' worth a darn, and I finally had to let him go. He tried to set fire to the barn 'fore he left! Thankfully I saw it, got it out 'fore it spread, but if I coulda got muh hands on him I'da wrung his worthless neck!" The others laughed, one waved the bartender over and ordered more drinks and asked about the Faro table, which prompted the men to leave the table and go to the Faro game.

Cord left the mug half full, turned away, and walked out of the bar, pushing through the swinging doors, and stepping into the full daylight. A man was seated in the shade of the overhang and leaned back against the building as Cord stepped through the doors. He stopped when he saw a man, one of the three he spotted at the first bar, reaching to the saddlebags on Kwitcher and beginning to undo the flap strap. At the thug's feet, Blue came alive, growling and the man kicked at him, laughing. Cord stepped down from the boardwalk, and unseen, moved behind the man as he reached up to lift the flap.

Cord grabbed the back of the would-be thief's hand, pulled him close, and with both his hands around the startled man's wrist, thumbs on the back of his hand, Cord raised his hands high, and brought the gripped hand down with a hard jerk. The man screamed as he heard the bone in his arm crack and break. He dropped to his knees, holding his arm, and looked up at Cord. But Cord's attention had turned to another one of the three ne-er do wells that had stepped forward and hollered at Cord as he was grabbing for the pistol holstered at his side. Blue leaped to the man, sinking his teeth into the thug's calf, but Cord had taken a long step to the hitchrail, snatched his pistol from the holster, and brought the barrel down on the man's neck, knocking him to the ground, unconscious. Cord called, "Blue!" and the dog released his grip and came to Cord's side, blood dripping from his teeth, and stood beside his master. Cord was certain these were the same men at the end of the first bar who talked to the bartender.

He slipped Kwitcher's reins and the mule's lead rope from the hitchrail and glanced at the seated

man who had not stirred during the ruckus. He heard
the man say, "That's a fine lookin' horse you got
there; good dog too. Neither one of 'em paid any
attention to passersby until one stumblin' drunk
came near to fallin' on the hitchrail an' and that dog
came off the ground, lowered his head, and growled
at the drunk, sent him on his way he did!" declared
the man, laughing. "You give those two," nodding to
the two men on the ground—"just what they
needed. They been askin' for it for quite a spell. I'm
thankin' you for that!"

Cord just grinned, although it didn't show
through his whiskers, nodded, and mounted up to
leave. He was glad to put Lawrence behind him, but
he thought he would try to find the freighter wagons,
see about that job as a hunter. He did not need the
money, but it would make travel a little safer. He had
heard about some of the reservation Indians causing
some trouble and he knew most of the native peoples
further west were still making themselves known
with raids and more.

8

FREIGHTERS

CORD GUESSED IT WAS ABOUT THREE TO FOUR MILES SOUTH of Lawrence when he spotted the camp of the freighters on the far side of Wakarusa River. Before him lay the bridge known as Blanton's Bridge, although it was not the original. Scars of black marred the nearby trees that told of the burning of the bridge a few years back by the raiders of Quantrill as they left the city in smoke and ashes, but the bridge, like Lawrence, had been rebuilt and stood proudly across the river, another symbol of the determination and character of the people of Lawrence. He nudged Kwitcher to the bridge and the hooves of the big stallion and the mule clattered across the planks as he pointed his animals to the freighters camp. As he neared, he counted the wagons, saw there were ten wagons, each in a double hookup, and a large herd of mules grazing between the wagons and the river.

He hailed the camp as he neared and was answered by a man that stepped around a wagon, holding a rifle across his chest, "What's your business?" he growled. Cord reined up, leaned on his pommel as he sized up the man before him. He was a big man, a little over six feet, probably two hundred twenty pounds, bearded and balding head, scowling expression and wearing canvas britches held up by overworked galluses that stretched over a linsey Woolsey shirt that hadn't seen water or soap probably since it was made. Hobnail boots showed from under the hem and Cord's attention was arrested when the man levered a round into the chamber of the rifle and repeated, "I said, what's your business?!"

"I was told in town your ramrod was lookin' for workers - muleskinners, swampers and a hunter," replied Cord.

"Which're you?"

"Hunter."

"Stay here, I'll be back with the wagonmaster."

Cord sat up, looked about, saw the wagons all appeared to be in good repair, all with heavier than normal wheels and undercarriages, high sideboards, and canvas tops over wooden hoops. Two of the wagons differed, one was obviously a water wagon, the other he guessed to be a cook wagon. His attention was caught when the men returned and the second man, a little older than the first and with a clean-shaven face, linen shirt over canvas britches, boots, and a felt hat. He looked up at Cord, "Step down, let's talk!"

As Cord complied, he stood beside Kwitcher and extended his hand, "I'm Cordell Beckett. The bartender in town said you were lookin' for a hunter?"

"I'm Major Russell, Mickey Russell, I'm the wagonmaster. You reckon yourself to be a hunter?"

"That's right."

"I'll have twenty to twenty-five men that know how to eat, and they want their supper on time. The cook needs the meat ready, well before time to cook, preferably the day before. That means about fifty pounds of meat a day, which is about half a deer. Of course they would like a little variety to their meals, you know, different meats, maybe fish, birds, and such. Think you could handle that?"

Cord nodded. Glanced to the other man that was scowling and fidgety, then back to the wagonmaster.

"If I take you on, you'll be paid the same as a muleskinner, and hungry men will give you no slack, and Cooky - the way he thinks, if you don't provide the meat, he'll slice you up into steaks and put you on the platter," declared the wagonmaster, showing no humor in his expression.

"When you pullin' out?" asked Cord.

"First light."

"Where you bound?"

"Santa Fe Trail —takin' freight to Fort Zarah,

Dodge, Larned, Lyon. The trip will take us 'bout a month, mebbe more."

"You pickin' up the meat or is Cooky?"

"You bring it into the train or leave it where it'll be safe and easy to pick it up. Don't matter who's gettin' it."

Cord glanced to the lowering sun, guessed there to be about two hours of light before total darkness, and knew this would be a good time for hunting. He looked back to the major, "If it's all right with you, I'll head out now, maybe get somethin' 'fore dark." He looked about, "That the cook wagon?" nodding toward the one wagon with canvas top that was a little smaller than the others.

"It is."

"I'll drop it there."

"When you do, I'll have a map for you, so you won't get too far afield of the trail."

Cord nodded, stabbed his boot into the stirrup, and swung aboard. Reined the stallion around and started past the wagons, moving upstream on the Wakarusa, staying at the edge of the trees. He moved slowly across the low rolling terrain, wide-open fields showed green grasses waving in the evening breeze, but he stayed near the tree line that followed the river. He had traveled about a mile and a half before coming to the confluence of a little feeder creek that dumped into the Wakarusa. The trees were thinner and the breaks irregular, perfect for animals coming to water. He reined up next to the trees, stood in his stirrups to look toward the feeder creek, and as suspected, he saw movement. Three deer, white-tails, were moving through the thin trees, making their way to the creek.

Cord stepped down, ground tied the horse and mule, and with the Henry at the ready, he moved into the trees to begin his stalk. Within moments, he spotted the deer, saw one to be a good-sized buck, the second a doe, and the third a younger buck, although it was unusual for the doe to be with two bucks at this time of year. Carefully watching their movements, he waited until they were at the creek, none looking his way, and moved a little closer. When about forty yards away, he went to one knee, used his upright knee for a leaning rest, and took aim at the larger buck. He dropped the hammer and the quiet of the evening and the woods was shattered by the blast of the Henry, and he jacked another round and followed the young buck as it turned back from the water and lifted his front end to take flight, but the second round from the Henry sounded before the echo of the first drifted away. And both bucks were on the ground as the doe flashed her white tail and disappeared into the trees.

Cord moved quickly to the downed bucks, nudged each one, and satisfied, stood the Henry beside a nearby tree, and withdrew his Bowie knife and slit the throats of each one to let them bleed out. He split them from tail to nose, dragged out the innards, and soon had the animals field dressed, but he cut off the legs and heads, left them with the gut piles and lay the big buck over the mule, the smaller behind the cantle of his saddle, tied them down, and was soon on his way back to the wagons.

As he rode into the camp, he was halted by the lookout, recognized, and allowed to ride into the area near the cook wagon. Two fires were blazing, one encircled by the men with plates in their laps, the other with a metal tripod holding a massive coffee pot and a grill with a huge frying pan. He reined up and walked to the cookfire, looked at the man tending the frying pan and said, "I'm Cord. I've got some meat for you."

The man looked up, slid the frying pan away from the flames, and stood, wiping his hands on his already dirty apron. He removed a pipe from his mouth and looked at Cord, "So, you're the hunter, are you?"

Cord nodded, pointing to the horse and mule packing the deer carcasses, "Where you want 'em?"

"I'm Cooky," declared the man, giving his hands another wipe on his apron, grinned and extended his hand to Cord.

Cord shook hands, "I'm Cord."

Cooky grinned, nodding and walked to the animals, looked at the carcasses, back to Cord, "Just get 'em?"

Cord nodded, waiting for an answer.

Cooky said, "You gonna skin 'em?"

"I will those I bring into camp, providin' there's time."

"Then get at it boy!" declared the grinning cook. "I'll get you some coffee." He pointed to the far side of the cook wagon, "There's room o'er there."

9

BURLINGAME

CORD MADE HIS CAMP APART FROM THE WAGONS, preferring a solitary retreat in the trees, but he was up before the men and had his animals geared and ready as he led them into the camp to have his breakfast with the others. Smoke rose from the cookfire where Cooky busied himself and his helper tending the tasty strip steaks that hung over the fire with long tongued flames licking at the strips and swallowing every drip of melted fat. The big coffee pot hung from the tripod over the grill and the lid bounced as the steam escaped from the spout and lifted the lid. Men of all sorts were making their way to the fire, most rubbing the sleep from their eyes as they stumbled near, squinting at the brighter light of the fire, and wading through the drifting smoke.

Cord glanced at each one, seeing little difference. Most with stubbles of whiskers, dirty faces, and tattered clothes, the non-descript men found a seat around the fire, mumbling greeting to one another as they waited for their breakfast. The uniform of the teamsters appeared to be canvas trousers held in place with galluses, linsey Woolsey shirts, hobnail boots, and tattered long johns showing at all the gaps where buttons strained to do their job of holding things together. None of the men acknowledged Cord, most giving him a cursory glance, maybe a nod, but none offered a greeting. When Major Russell came to the circle, he too nodded to Cord, and glanced to Cooky as he growled, "Coffee ready?"

Without an answer, Cooky lifted the heavy pot from the hook, handed it to his helper, who started around the circle with a string of cups dangling from his belt allowing each man to pick a cup and hold it steady for the shaky hand of the cook's helper to fill it full of the steaming brew. Cord took a cup and was pleased with the black brew, strong enough to wake a man from his drowsing, hot enough to burn his lip. Cord stood, left his cup on the tailgate of the wagon, grabbed up a couple of sizzling strips of meat, and swung aboard his horse. With a nod to the major, Cord rode from the camp with the sun splitting the darkness and making way for the shadows of the eastern horizon.

———

WITH THE RISING sun warming his back, Cord straddled the carcass of the white-tail buck he killed at the edge of the trees by the creek. He had agreed with Cooky to hang any carcass from a tree limb near the trail, tie a strip of white cloth from it so it could be easily spotted, and they would pick it up as they passed. Cord chuckled as he field-dressed the deer, thinking about Cooky putting his helper, Squirt, to work skinning and cutting up the carcasses. He tried to get Cord to do the skinning, but Cord convinced him that the meat would be best if the skin was left on until they picked it up, keeping the flies and such from the meat. He quickly finished his task, dragged the carcass well away from the gut pile, and picked out a tree with a sturdy branch that would be visible from the trail, hoisted the carcass up, tied it off, and hung the strip of cloth that would wave in the wind and attract the attention of the passing teamsters and Cooky.

He was pleased with the abundance of game in this land of rolling hills, grassy plains and plenty of waterways that enticed the game to congregate in the early morning and evening hours, making them easy targets for Cord. After washing off the blood and guts, and cleaning his knife and rifle, he went to the tethered animals, tightened the girths, and swung aboard. It was still early in the day and the wagons would be along shortly, but Cord had no desire to travel with the train and took to the trail to make time while the sun was high. According to the crude map provided by the major, the next town would be Burlingame, and he calculated he would be there about mid-day tomorrow. Although they did not plan a stop there, he wanted to go into the town and see if there was any news of the Red Leg renegades.

Cord shivered as he climbed up the bank from the deep pool in the bend of the creek. He wiped off the excess water, shook it free from his hair, and reached for the blanket to dry himself. The dip in the creek felt good, it had been a while, and he was in dire need of some cleanness. He chuckled as he remembered the oft repeated remonstrance of his mother about his reluctance to take a bath. He slipped on his clean clothes and stood before the mirror hanging on the tree branch. The mirror was one of the few things he salvaged from the ruins of his family home; it was his mother's and was a simple mirror in a metal frame with a short handle, suitable for sticking in a fork of a branch and standing upright. He lathered up his hands with the bar of lye soap, wiped it on his neck and cheeks, and after stropping his razor on the girth strap of his saddle, he began to shave. He was only trimming his beard, shaving mostly his neck and upper cheeks, preferring to keep his full face of whiskers, believing it made him look older.

Satisfied, he turned to the creek, went to one knee and splashed water on his face, cleaned the razor and his hands and paused when he heard what sounded like a giggle coming from behind him. He carefully folded the razor, slipped it into his pocket, glanced to the side, and slowly turned around, his hand on the butt of his holstered pistol. Standing beside the big trunk of a Hackberry tree stood a young native woman, her hand to her mouth to stifle the giggle and her eyes dancing in laughter.

"Well, hello! Who're you?" he asked, looking at the girl who he guessed to be about fourteen summers.

She was pretty with her raven black hair, clean and shiny, hanging free over her shoulders. Her trim figure showed a blossoming body covered with a beaded tunic with fringed leggings underneath. She smiled, turned, and ran into the woods, and before Cord could follow, he heard the muted rumble of a running horse as she disappeared beyond the trees. Cord chuckled, shook his head, and finished gearing up. With a glance over his shoulder in the direction the young woman disappeared, he nudged Kwitcher from the clearing into the open of the flat grassland to greet the rising sun of another day.

The simple sign stood lonely on the edge of the road, tilted slightly to the side, and read Burlingame, apparently telling of the town that was next on the trail. The rolling hills and wide grassy flats offered no clues of a nearby town, but the swales between the hillocks could easily hide the typical town of this area. Cord grinned at the thought of a town hiding itself but as he crested the nearest hill, the long slope beyond ended in the many structured town of

Burlingame. He pushed on and as he entered the village, he looked about, surprised at the many structures of stone. In the middle of the town center, a communal well stood proudly, the well housing sheltered with a peaked cover that shielded the crank and bucket. Cord looked at the different businesses, saw the usual hotel, saloons, livery, barber, gunsmith, and mercantile. He reined up before the mercantile, stepped down and slapped Kwitcher's rein over the hitchrail and did the same with the lead rope of the mule. He motioned to Blue to stay with the animals and stepped up on the boardwalk and entered the mercantile.

He paused in the doorway, letting his eyes adjust to the dim interior, stepped to the side, and started to the counter. A middle-aged tall woman stood behind the counter, watched Cord approach and with a stoic expression she asked, "Can I help you?"

"Yes'm," answered Cord, tipping his hat to the lady, "if you would. I need some coffee, salt, sugar, cornmeal, flour, and some .44 ammunition. Here's a list I wrote out." He lay the crumpled paper on the counter and leaned against the top.

The woman accepted the list, turned away, and began gathering the goods. Cord watched, looking around the interior as he stood, arms crossed on his chest. The woman was very efficient, wasting no moves nor time and soon had everything stacked on the counter. She looked up at Cord, "Will that be all?"

"Yes'm, thank you," answered Cord and continued, "Say, ma'am, do you mind if I ask you a question?"

"You just did, but go ahead," she responded as she tallied up the cost of the goods.

"Have you folks had any trouble lately, you know, from a band of renegades posing as Red Legs?"

She stopped what she was doing, frowned up at Cord. "I'll have you know my husband was a Red Leg and proud of it!"

Cord stammered, "That's not what I meant, ma'am. This is a bunch of renegades that aren't really Red Legs, they just make out like they are and when folks drop their guard, they raise all kinds of trouble. The sheriff up in Douglas County asked me to keep a watch out for any sign of 'em and to let him know if I come across anything."

She frowned, glaring at Cord, "What's the sheriff's name, the one up in Douglas County?"

"Sam Walker, he was sheriff 'fore the war and now again. Those fellas have been causin' problems up thataway, leave for a couple months, then come back and do it all again. That's why he wanted me to keep an eye out for 'em." He paused, glancing about, "You see ma'am, I'm scoutin' an' huntin' for a wagon train of freighters owned by Butterfield, and we're headin' west, and he thought I might see 'em or hear about 'em, that's all."

She huffed, growled, "That'll be three dollars an'

twenty-five cents! And I ain't seen nor heard 'bout no renegades!"

Cord nodded, dug in his pocket for some coin, counted them out on the counter, and looked at the woman, "I didn't mean no offense, ma'am," he said softly, looking at the woman, his dark eyes peering from under the brim of his hat as he gathered up his goods.

"I'm sorry, young man, we've had more'n our share of trouble 'round here. During the war, Bloody Bill Anderson was from just down the road an' he promised to burn our town. We been kinda skittish since 'fore the war."

"I understand, ma'am," nodded Cord, he paused, "Is there a band of natives nearby?"

"Why?"

Cord chuckled, "I saw one back in the trees by the river a bit outta town. Just for a minute, then she rode off."

The woman slowly let a smile split her face and asked, "A woman?"

Cord chuckled, "A right pretty one too."

"Probably Potawatomie. There's a band of 'em north of here, peaceful folks."

"Thank you, ma'am," replied Cord, smiling at the woman, even though she couldn't tell it with his face full of whiskers, but he tipped his hat and left.

10

COUNCIL GROVE

VAST MEADOWS AND ROLLING PLAINS THICK WITH bluestem, gramma, buffalo grass and more seemed to stretch into oblivion every time he crested a slight hill. Beyond each rise were the tops of trees that stretched to the blue sky as he moved over each crest, and the trees harbored creek after creek. He had traveled the rest of the day after leaving Burlingame across the repetitive land and as the sun set before him, he was relieved to see the end of the long day approaching as he came to another line of trees that undoubtedly hid another creek like all the others. As he rode into the thickets of maples, oaks, elms, and box elders, he spotted a nice clearing where the sun still shone through the break in the trees that offered access to the chuckling waters of the stream.

He reined up, leaning on his pommel as he looked around. Satisfied, he spoke to Kwitcher, "Well, boy, looks like we found us a camp," and swung down to step in the deep grass and begin stripping the animals of their gear. He glanced to the side to see Blue bounding away probably after a rabbit and shook his head as he remembered the many times he and his dad had gone into the woods hunting rabbits, but that was long ago and far away.

He stacked the gear under a wide branching hackberry, stripped off his duster, and lay it atop the gear, then led the animals to the creek for some water. He saw tracks of deer, fox, coyote, and turkey. He looked about, listening, searching the woods for any sign or movement, but there was only the sounds of distant birds and nearby squirrels that were a mite agitated at the interloper to their domain and scolded him accordingly. He had thus far provided the wagon train with ample meat, finding it easy to bag deer both early morning and evening. But he had been watching for anything that would provide a change and although he had seen antelope at a distance, he had not been fortunate enough to get near them for a shot.

He walked back to the clearing, the horse and mule following, and once picketed, they began to graze. Cord began to gather some wood for his fire and listened to the songbirds. He recognized the repeated trill of the meadowlark, the mournful call of the dove, and the rattling hammering of the wood-pecker. When the red-winged blackbird gave its alarming call, the others fell silent until the cowbird gave its chirp, chirp, tweet, and the others resumed their songs. Cord grinned as he built his fire, remembering his mother as she would sit in the wicker rocker on their porch, knitting, and listening to the birds. He smiled as he remembered her words about the meadowlark, "Don't you hear that? He said *Peter went to Sunday school!*" and would let a soft giggle escape without ever missing a move in her knitting. He sighed heavily, sadness sweeping over him at the many memories that refused to give him any reprieve.

He thought of his father, standing firm and stoic in the pulpit, his open Bible in his hand and his free hand uplifted, "God never fails! Sometimes we expect God to do our bidding, make everything nice an easy and when He doesn't do what we want, we are tempted to think He does not care! But He does care, more than we can comprehend, and He never fails! Deuteronomy 31:6 tells us, *Be strong and of a good courage, fear not, nor be afraid of them: for The Lord thy God, he it is that doth go with thee; he will not fail thee, nor forsake thee.*"

Cord grumbled, looked to the heavens, and shook his hand, "He failed me! What about that, huh, Dad? Where was God when those Red Legs hit our home? Answer me that!" He realized he was yelling and stopped, looked around to see Kwitcher with his head lifted and looking at him, the mule also. The birds had stopped their singing and even the squirrel had scampered into his den. A few trees shook their leaves at the recalcitrant man as if they were scolding him, and Cord dropped his fist, shook his head, and stomped to the gear to get the supper makings. But when he spotted his fishing rig, he grinned, grabbed the reel and line, hooks, and headed to the creek to get a willow, dig some worms, and try to catch some fish for his supper.

———

HE LAY BACK, hands behind his head, satisfied with a full stomach filled with the fried filets of white crappie and cornbread, and looked at the stars. It was a clear night, the air cool, and some birds were lifting their songs to the night. Although he knew some of the songs came from a mockingbird, the distant drumming of the loon and the nearer questions of the night came from an owl, probably a Barred owl. Yet he enjoyed nature's lullaby, as it kept his thoughts off what had been his time of prayer. Although he had tried to pray since the raid, he found it difficult and the memories hard to renew, and his frustration, anger, and disappointment always crowded out the thoughts of prayer. With the distant deep-throated call of a loon, Cord drifted off to sleep.

Cord was brought rudely awake with the squawk, squawk, gobble of a tom turkey. He looked about, trying to locate the source of aggravation, but he was not in the clearing, but further into the woods, probably nearer the creek. Cord breathed deep, crawled from his blankets in the dim light of early morn, and went to the pack to retrieve his Parker coach gun, the double-barreled 10-gauge would quiet that Tom, he thought, chuckling as he pulled it from the sheath, grabbed a handful of shells and started in the direction of the bird, stepped on a branch, and winced, having forgotten his boots. He shook his head at his own foolishness, quickly slipped on his boots, and started into the trees.

He moved quietly, listening for the squawk and gobble of the tom, and picked his steps carefully, using the grasses, moss, and wet leaves to mask his approach. He peeked through the edge of the trees to a marshy clearing with the creek on one side and a wide meadow on the other. A flock of turkeys were gathered under a lonesome tree, and several big toms were strutting about, showing off for the hens. At least one hen had a handful of poults near, but the others were off to one side, watching the entertainment as the toms strutted, gobbling, yelping, purring, and clucking. The toms with their red wattles and long beards were competing and paying little attention to anything else. Cord used the cover of trees and brush to move closer and pick his target. He knew it would take more than one turkey to feed the men of the wagon train and if he was going to get one, he better get more.

He lifted the Parker, the hammers already cocked, and he thought out his shots. He dropped the hammer, and the 10-gauge roared and bucked, spitting a cloud of smoke, but Cord quickly swung the muzzle to his left, dropped the second hammer, and lowered the weapon to break open the breach and reload. He quickly lifted the big gun, saw another tom trotting away, and dropped the hammer again, then a trailing hen, all alone, was the last to fall.

Cord let the smoke clear and the ruckus settle before he left the brush. As he came to the downed birds, he was pleased as he lifted each one, surprised to see his first shot had taken two birds, apparently two competing toms. He looked about, guessing there would be about forty to fifty, pounds of meat, or more, total with the five birds. He quickly gutted the birds, looked for a tree that would offer a good branch that would be visible from the trail and lifted his daily bounty high off the ground, trailing the long strip of white cloth to catch the attention of the ever-vigilant Cooky.

It was mid-morning when he took to the trail, and by late afternoon, after crossing another four creeks, he came to the town of Council Grove, which straddled the Neosho River. As he rode down the main street, he saw several stone and brick buildings, the most prominent being the Hays House, a restaurant that seemed to call his name. Although the businesses seem to be many and covering several blocks, he resisted the urge to keep moving, and decided to stop. He grinned as he nudged Kwitcher to the hitchrail and stepped down, pointing to the ground at the stallion's feet for Blue to lay, and with the animals secured, he stepped onto the boardwalk, used his hat to slap the dust from his clothes, replaced the felt hat, and stepped into the restaurant.

He was greeted by a pretty young woman with a white lacy apron covering her blue striped dress wearing a wide smile as she said, "Welcome to the Hays House. Won't you be seated, and I'll bring you some coffee while you decide what you would like." She waved her hand to the open tables, turned away, and started to the kitchen area, leaving Cord to decide where to be seated. He chose the lone table near the big bay window and seated himself, doffed his hat, placed it on the chair beside him, and looked about.

It was a pleasant place, several tables held other diners, most paying little attention to the lone man by the window. He looked out the window at the main street, saw a hotel, a mercantile and more businesses, but there was not a lot of activity for such a sizable town. His reverie was interrupted when the girl brought his coffee cup, poured it full, and asked, "Have you decided what you would like?"

Cord looked at the young woman, nodded, and asked, "What do you recommend?"

She smiled and said, "Our special this evening is beef steak with potatoes and gravy and fresh vegetables."

"That sounds wonderful, I'll have that," answered Cord as the woman nodded, smiled, and left for the kitchen.

When she returned with his plate of food, she sat it down, stepped back and with a smile, and asked, "Will there be anything else?"

"Just a question. For such a good-sized town, it seems awful quiet. Is it always this way?"

She relaxed, stepped a little closer, "Mostly, but not always. They're building the railroad this way, and whenever some of those men come into town, it can get a little rowdy. But you know, they work hard and need some time to let off some steam, at least that's what most folks say."

"Is that all? What about all that ruckus that was goin' on durin' and after the war?"

She frowned, looking around to see if anyone was paying them any attention, and leaned forward, "You mean like, you know, the raiders and such?"

"Ummhmm, I heard there was some trouble with 'em back toward Lawrence. The sheriff up to Douglas County asked me to keep a look out for any of 'em. He said they cause trouble there, leave, and come back a couple months later. I'm scouting for a wagon train of freighters comin' through and he thought I might let him know if I heard anything."

"Oh, I see. I understand. Well...," she paused, looked about and continued, "a few weeks back, maybe more'n a month now, there was a bunch that came through, real rough lookin', and they came to town the same time some of the railroaders did, and boy was there trouble! The sheriff threw a bunch of 'em in jail, run the others outta town, but they busted up a couple saloons and more before they left."

"Did you hear any names?"

She frowned again, looking about nervously, "All I heard was one of the leaders of the bunch was called Doc sumthin'."

Cord nodded, looked at the other diners, and smiled at the girl. "Thank you. You better go. I think some of the others are getting antsy."

She nodded, turned away, and went to a table where a man was waving, and lifted his coffee cup for some more brew. She nodded, started for the kitchen, and glanced back over her shoulder at Cord, smiled, and disappeared into the kitchen.

Cord pulled his plate closer as he lifted his knife and fork, thinking about the names that had been branded into his memory and was remembering one man who was thought to be a leader named Charles "Doc" Jennison. He thought this was his first real lead and believed he was on the right trail, he looked at his food, grinned and began to enjoy the meal, satisfied with his progress.

11

VISITORS

CORD'S REVERIE AS HE ATE WAS RUDELY INTERRUPTED when he saw a man driving a buckboard come roaring into town behind a lathered team screaming and shouting, "Indians! Indians! Indians!" The people on the street hurriedly gathered about, asking questions and breaking away to run tell others or to find shelter. The man jumped from his wagon and ran into the Hays House, stood in the doorway and shouted, "Indians! Indians! Run or arm yourselves!" and turned away to carry his alarm along the street and to the other businesses.

A table nearer the door held four men, all wearing business attire, and they seemed especially agitated. One turned to the man with his back to the door, a gentleman of about fifty years, dignified with a trim moustache, long sideburns, all showing touches of grey, and dark eyes that seemed to nail his companions to their chairs, each leaning slightly toward the man. The smaller of the four spoke up, "What're we gonna do, Seth?"

"Easy gentlemen, easy." He paused, looked at each man, and nodded to one, "Horace, you run down to the livery, tell Joe Jim to go to Topeka and ask the governor for help." The man jumped to his feet and ran from the room, slamming the door open and his footsteps could be heard pounding down the boardwalk. Seth chuckled, shaking his head, "Simpson, you gather the merchants together, we need to meet right away, here in the lobby," nodding to the lobby of the adjoining hotel. Simpson rose to his feet and hurried away. Seth looked to the last man, "Curtis, you go to the sheriff, tell him to round up as many men as he can, armed, and meet in the circle!"

Curtis nodded, and quickly walked from the room.

Cord had watched the hustle and bustle, not only in the Hays House, but on the streets outside. He finished his meal, stood, and went to the counter to pay for his meal and looked at the man referred to as Seth and stepped near, "I take it you're the leader of this community?"

The older man looked up at Cord, who stood near with his hat brim turned down and his dark eyes showing from the shadow, and the man answered, "You could say that. My name is Seth Hays. I'm one of the first settlers in this area and you are standing in my business, The Hays House."

"This Indian attack doesn't seem to have you too upset. Do you get many?"

"No, not many. The Kaw or Kansa people have their reservation nearby and they are usually a peaceful people, but they've been enemies with the Cheyenne and the Cheyenne have been known to make raids on the Kaw, and on white settlements. So, my guess is, the alarm has to do with some Cheyenne. We'll just have to be prepared and see what happens. Now," he rose from his seat, stood looking at Cord, "if you will excuse me, I must meet with some of the other leaders of the community."

Cord nodded, stepped back to let the man pass, and followed him from the restaurant, but stopped on the boardwalk, and looked up and down the street. People were hustling about, men escorting women from the stores to homes or wagons to leave the town. He noticed most of the men carrying rifles as they tended to their chores, and Cord decided to go to the livery before deciding what he would do or not. He stepped aboard Kwitcher and with the lead rope in hand, he started to the west end of the street where he had seen the livery.

He reined up at the big door under the sign that read Council Livery, P.B. Roberts, owner. As Cord looked into the shadowy interior a man hurried from the livery, leading a less than eager horse and followed by a youngster of about eight already mounted and pushing his horse close behind the other. They were followed by a man Cord assumed to be the smithy as he wore a leather apron with a stained front, carried a set of tongs, and talked to the man, "Now Joe Jim, you get a move on, if you wanna leave the boy, I'll see to it he's cared for."

"No, P.B., he's comin' with me. His gran'pa expects me to teach him ever'thin' I know, so this is as good a way to learn as any. 'Sides, he's a better rider'n I am an' we're goin' through his land!" He chuckled as he swung aboard his mount. He looked at the boy, "You ready, Charley?"

The boy grinned, nodded, and kicked his short legs against the ribs of his horse and took off to the northeast.

The smithy stood, watching the pair ride away, shaking his head and mumbling. Cord asked, "He the one goin' to Topeka?"

The smithy jumped as he turned to face Cord, "Din't see'ya thar. Skeered me, you did."

He looked at Cord, "You need somethin'?"

"Dunno. I heard the warnin' about Indians comin', thought I'd stop by here and get your take on the doin's." He nodded to the retreating pair, "Ain't that a little careless, takin' a boy like that on a ride like that, it's what, three days or so to Topeka?"

The smithy chuckled, "That's Indian Charley, his real name is Charles Curtis[1]; he's part Kaw Indian himself and has been raised by his grandparents who live on the reservation with their people. And like Joe Jim said, Charley's a better rider than him and him bein' along will make it

easier to get across the res without gettin'
stopped."

"So, what do you think is gonna happen?"

"Since they're comin' from the northwest, they're
probably Cheyenne, an' more'n likely they'll be goin'
after the Kaw. But it never hurts to be ready, so, that
bein' said, if you don't need nothin' more, I'm gonna
go get my rifle and take to my loft." He turned on his
heel and disappeared into the shadowy interior
without another word to Cord.

Cord leaned down and stroked the neck of
Kwitcher, glanced to the mule, and down to Blue,
"Well, fellas, either we join the smithy or we find us a
good spot in the woods somewhere, but I think it
might be best to stay here, so..." He swung down and
led the animals into the livery, found a couple empty
stalls and loosened the girths on the saddles, gave
them water and a flake of hay, called Blue into
Kwitcher's stall and told him to stay as he took his
Henry and a pouch of ammo and went to the ladder
to join the smithy in the loft. The smithy turned as
Cord mounted the ladder, nodded, and turned back
to the big loft window; he was belly down on the
loose hay and Cord joined him.

Cord stretched out just as P.B. motioned, "There
they come!" pointing to a crowd of riders coming
from the northwest. As they neared the town, one of
the leaders motioned to the others and the group
split with half going to the south edge of the town
and the rest continuing on the trail that turned into

the main street of the village. Cord frowned as he looked at the large bunch, he guessed there were a good hundred warriors coming toward the town and the other bunch was of a little lesser size but still more than enough to wreak havoc in a battle.

He mumbled, "If they attack, we're in more trouble than most think!"

But before P.B. could answer, a voice called from below, "Hey P.B., Seth wants me to get that buckboard and team, take it behind the mercantile. Can you help me?"

"Sure Smitty! I'll be right down. You go fetch that team of blacks in the corral, I'll get the harness!" P.B. looked at Cord, "Wanna give me a hand?"

Cord nodded, came to his feet, and followed the smithy down the ladder. They made short work of the harnessing and the wagon pulled from the livery as Cord and P.B. returned to the loft. Cord asked, "Did he say they were gettin' together a peace offering?"

"Ummhmm, Seth figgers we might buy off them Cheyenne. Reckon it's worth a try. If'n it don't work, them redskins'll just take ever'thin' anyway, so we ain't got nuthin' to lose!"

They bellied down in the hay and watched the two bunches of natives ride into and around the town. Those coming into the town were led by three men, obviously chiefs of some sort, but all were arrayed in their finest regalia suitable for battle. With bone hairpipe breastplates, chokers, lances with feathers and scalplocks, painted and decorated buffalo hide war shields, head dresses and feathered scalplocks dangling from weapons and adorning their braided hair, they were a formidable looking band. Most had fringed buckskin leggings, breech-cloths, a few with beaded and fringed tunics, and all sat splendid mounts that had also been painted and decorated.

They rode through the town, scowling at the few people that peered out of windows, or doorways, and even though the people of the town showed their weapons, no one was eager to start the fight. The natives rode four and five side by side, with the entire band of about a hundred warriors, all bedecked in their finery and paint, filling up the entire street the length of the town. Two stately warriors, both with war bonnets, bone hairpipe breastplates, rode at the front, chests out, heads held high and proud. Cord asked, "Who are those two, the ones out front?"

P.B. chuckled, "That's Black Kettle and Tall Bull, both chiefs, both tough men!" It was obvious to everyone that there were enough natives to more than destroy the town and everyone there, and most did not even know about the additional hundred or so that had ridden south of the town.

Cord and P.B. lay silent, watching the parade of Cheyenne, every face stoic and few even looking at the many citizens, and the low rumble of the many hooves of the horses seemed to rattle every window and door in the village. As they rode from the town, a collective sigh of relief escaped not only P.B. but Cord as well, until they saw the wagon, now loaded with goods and driven by Smitty who sat with Seth, both having doffed their business attire and now wore the common clothing of a working man, linen shirt stuffed into canvas trousers, and both with Winchesters across their laps. They followed the bunch of Cheyenne that had ridden through town but kept their distance well behind the natives.

Cord and P.B. stood, taking a last look at the disappearing natives and the wagon with Seth and Smitty, then climbed down from the loft. Cord looked at P.B. and asked, "So, they think they can make a trade, those goods for peace?"

"That's what they're thinkin'."

"I'm gonna hafta see this," declared Cord, going to the stalls to retrieve his animals.

As he led them to the door and stepped aboard, P.B. followed and said, "You ain't any smarter'n them!" as he watched Cord grin, step aboard, and ride from the town.

12

FORT ZARAH

Cord kept to the trees and the lowlands, doing all he could to keep out of sight of the warriors, yet wanting to keep the wagon with Seth and Smitty in sight. When the natives crossed the river, they avoided the bridge, choosing to ford the shallow waters of the Neosho River, but the wagon driven by Smitty took the bridge and clattered over the planks and stopped on the far side.

As Cord came alongside, they looked up at the young man and Seth asked, "What're you doin' out here?"

"Thought I'd have a closer look-see. Wondered what you two were doin', but I can see you've got a load of goods there. Settin' up a trade, are you?"

Seth turned away from Cord, huffed as he crossed his arms in a dismissive gesture and motioned to Smitty to drive on. Cord shook his head at the arrogance of the man but was not surprised, he remembered his father saying, "Some folks are so full of themselves there ain't no room for anything like facts, truth, good judgment, and such. They think they're the only ones that know what's right. Now mind son, there are some folks that are very wise, but the only way to properly understand others, is to know the Bible. That's God's standard, all else falls short."

Cord shook his head, mumbling to the memory, "Not sure how that applies here, but..." and nudged Kwitcher to the trees at the edge of the rolling plains that lay before them. It was evident by the crushed grasses, that the Cheyenne warriors had bunched up and followed their leaders across the wide meadow of tall grass. The wide-open space slid over the distant knoll, dropped into the bottom beyond where the creek, known as Big John Creek, wound its way to the south.

Cord reined Kwitcher to the edge of the trees on the south edge of the rolling flats, and keeping under cover, continued toward what was setting up to be a battleground. When he gained the creek, he turned to the north, but soon stopped, not wanting to take the animals any closer, preferring to make his approach on foot.

With the Henry in hand and the pouch of ammo at his belt, Cord began his stealthy approach, but stealth was not necessary as the battle had commenced. He heard rifle shots, shouted war cries, screams, and more. He hustled through the trees until he came to a bit of a bluff that dropped into the creek bottom. At a crouch, he mounted the bluff and dropped to his belly as he neared the top. With a cautious look, he saw the battle, but he was surprised that it appeared to be as much a contest as a fight. There *were* rifle shots, but it appeared that those with rifles were shooting high, arrows and lances were loosed and thrown, but no warriors appeared to be falling.

The battle continued with warriors laying low on their mounts, many swinging off the side with hooked heels at the hip and a hand twisted in the mane, the warriors fired one-handed from under the neck of the horses, then swung away and returned to their people. Such displays of horsemanship were shown by both the Cheyenne and the Kaw, while other warriors stood to the side and launched arrows in a high arc toward their opponents, most falling just short. Cord watched, frowning, confused, *It looks like they're just competing in a contest, not fighting a battle.* As he watched, the displays continued, warriors approaching their opponents, horses running at full speed, some warriors sitting high, others laying low, all firing their weapons but no one falling. It was an amazing scene and Cord marveled at the outstanding horsemanship and more, but he soon grew tired and decided to leave, yet as he started to rise, he heard the lull in the commotion and looked to see from both sides, what appeared to be the leaders, riding side by side, and approaching one another. They stopped short of one another but within talking distance and apparently negotiated a truce. When the talking stopped, the leader of the Kaw, a man attired with what appeared to be a beaver pelt round brimless hat, a white man's style shirt and britches, but wrapped in a robe of an elk, the chief known as Allegawaho, turned to motion to those behind him. In a few moments, several of the men drove a small bunch of horses, maybe a dozen, toward the Cheyenne. When the horses crossed to the Cheyenne, both chiefs nodded, made sign with their hands, and turned back to their own people.

Cord continued to watch and when the Cheyenne followed their leaders, they all stopped when they came to the wagon driven by Smitty. Seth stood, greeted the chiefs, and motioned to the goods in the wagon, and after some talk, the chief motioned to one of his men who stepped down, went to the wagon, and climbed aboard as Seth and Smitty stepped down. As the two white men stood to the side, the native turned the wagon and followed his chiefs as they returned the way they came.

Cord laughed, *If that don't beat all. A phony war, and the winner gets a wagonload of goods. That was more like a county fair with all the contests and more. Humph, we had better fairs than that back home.* He returned to his animals, climbed aboard, and turned back to the west, bound for the trail that would take him west and eventually into the high country of the Rocky Mountains, but first there was the matter of feeding the teamsters and covering the country between here and there.

It was late morning when Cord resumed his journey, according to what P.B. had said, it was about a day's ride to Diamond Springs, and from there to Fort Zarah might be close to a week, hopefully a little less. The wagon train was making good time, covering between fifteen and twenty miles a day, due to the experienced wagonmaster, Major Mickey Russell, who insisted on rotating out the tired animals for fresh and kept the wagons on the move, even with the grumbling of the teamsters and their swampers. Cord had consistently provided ample meat and the last time he rode into the freighters camp, the cook had said it might be good for him to get a little less meat, "It's gittin' so we're spoilin' these mule skinners, they're gittin' too fat! So..." he shrugged, grinning as he cut more steaks from the backstrap of the last deer hung by Cord.

From Council Grove, it was about a day to Diamond Springs, another day to Lost Springs and Cord hung a carcass at each campsite. After leaving Lost Springs by the dim light of early morning, he rode into the dry land of the tall grass prairie that held the dry buffalo grass, more cholla and piñon, and dry gulches with nothing more than gravel. He dropped into one gulch after spotting a small herd of antelope and thought he would try for one of the elusive animals. He slipped the Sharps from the pack, checked the load, and leaving the animals picketed in the draw with a little shade from an overhanging piñon, began a stalk on foot, using the tall grasses, cholla, and sage for cover.

With his rifle slung at his back, he bellied down, crawled under the branches of a sage, and lifted the binoculars for a scan of the land and the herd. He spotted the herd buck, standing watch at the edge of the herd, four or five smaller bucks grazing, but watchful, and six or seven doe, several with spindly legged fawns. He guessed the distance to be just a little less than a hundred yards and he carefully slipped the Sharps around, stretched it out and readied his shot. He narrowed the sight to the front lower chest of the bigger buck, took a breath, let some out, and slowly squeezed off his shot.

The Sharps bucked, spat smoke and lead, and because the muzzle was close to the ground, the blast stirred up a cloud of dust. Cord came to his knees, binoculars in hand, and spotted a bunch of white rumps disappearing in the distance, and as the smoke cleared, he saw the downed buck on its side near a clump of sage. *Humm, got one anyway, maybe Cooky will be pleased with the change and the lesser meat, hopefully,* chuckled Cord as he stood and walked back to the animals, Blue close on his heels until he spotted a rabbit and took off in a chase. Cord shook his head, loosed the tethers of the animals, and climbed aboard to ride to the downed carcass and begin the work of field dressing the buck.

———

CORD WAITED until the trail came to another creek where there were ample trees nearby and offered a good place to hang the antelope carcass. Cooky had told him there was at least one of his hanging meats that had been taken by other travelers or wild animals so they agreed he would hang them higher and further from the trail if necessary, using the white strips to signal the nearby hanging. Fortunately, antelope are smaller than the typical deer and he was able to hang it high and out of sight, leaving a small strip near the trail, another at the lower hanging branch of the tree. Satisfied, he mounted up and rode into the cooler air of dusk as he continued west.

Another day, another deer. Another day and two more deer. And so it went for the rest of the week until he saw a crude sign pointing the way to Fort Zarah. It was mid-afternoon when he neared the fort and had to stop to take a long look at the imposing structure that resembled the pictures he had seen of medieval castles in the old country, more than his pre-conceived image of a western military fort. The sandstone structures stood lonely on the desert. One was set apart to the southeast that looked to be about fourteen feet square with small windows high up and a single door that faced the fort. To the west of the main buildings was another smaller building, maybe twenty feet away and was about twelve feet square with no windows and a fortified door. But the main building is what captured Cord's attention, well over a hundred feet long and maybe fifty feet wide, the two-story structure of milled sandstone stood imposing with thin firing ports on each side and a hexagonal tower to the northeast and another identical tower to the southwest, also with several thin and tall firing ports on each side. Cord had never seen anything like it, and he sat leaning on his pommel, pushed his hat back and looked the sight over, taking in this unusual sight in the middle of nowhere.

Just to the east of the big fort, Cord saw a patch of blackened land that instantly brought back the memories of his family farm and he nudged Kwitcher forward, wanting to look it over. The recalcitrant mule was hesitant and dug in his heels, but Cord dallied the lead rope around the horn and Kwitcher leaned into his task, surprising the mule and they moved down the slight slope to make their way to Walnut Creek and the burned-out site of the Rath Ranch, a trading post marked on the map given to Cord by the major.

13

ARKANSAS RIVER

RED CLARK SAT STEWING, GROWLING, AND MUMBLING TO himself, staring at the cookfire as Newt Morrison pushed the bacon about and kept bumping the frying pan into the coffeepot. Red growled, "You spill that coffee and I'll spill you over the bluff yonder, right into that crick, mebbe wash off some o' that dirt and smell!"

Newt growled back, "Smell? If there's a stink in yore nostrils, it's your own stink!" He mumbled something else to himself, glared at Red, then glanced to the others, "An' if'n you don' like it, cook yore own supper!" He banged the pan into the pot again, venting some of his frustration and anger.

They were all frustrated and angry, this had been one of the worst days of their jaunt. Their usual practice was to take what they wanted from either travelers or settlers, and they had passed no travelers and the last two farms had already been hit by Indians, leaving them nothing but ashes to pick through and nothing to show for the last three days, and now they were on the last of their supplies.

"I still don't see why we had to leave Pitts behind, we coulda got him outta that place, he just din't know what he was doin'!" grumbled James Flood, looking around at the others to agree with him.

"That worthless good-for-nuthin' drunk was more trouble any ten men. He ain't worth the trouble! I tol' him if he went to that hog farm outside o' Fort Larned, he'd get hisself in trouble n' he sho'nuff did!" growled Red, glaring at Flood and glancing to the others. "And if'n I hear any more about it, I'll dump you off some'eres where nobody'll find you!"

Flood mumbled just loud enough for those nearby to hear, "I wish Doc or Jim was still here, they would'na left him!" But he knew Pitts had a penchant for women and a taste for whiskey, and most forts had a hog farm nearby where some whiskey peddler had women that sold themselves to any soldier or passersby that had the money and the time.

Jerry Malcolm hissed at the little man, "Better watch yore 'sef, Red is as likely to slit your throat as listen to your complainin'! 'Sides, you know Pitts couldn't resist no wimmen nor whiskey, an' when he had both, he was wuthless!"

Jack Hays, the biggest of the bunch but the slowest, looked at Flood, "Don' worry, Jim, ain't nobody gonna bother you. I won' let Red slit yo' throat!" and grunted as he grinned. Jack and Jim were inseparable, with Jack being the enforcer and Jim being the thinker of the pair. With his constant protector at his side, it sometimes made Flood a little braver and more vocal than was good for either of them, but tonight he chose to keep his opinions to himself.

The raggedy band of former Red Legs had lost their two leaders after their last raid on Harrisonville, Missouri, where they hit several outlying farms and took their plunder, leaving behind nothing but dead bodies and smoldering homes. That raid had been after the war was over, but they still thought they were fighting against slavery and Missouri was a slave state. Although none of these men were champions of the anti-slavery issue, they had used the guise of the Red Legs to fulfill their lust for violence and plunder. And they had done very little for the cause, choosing instead to take whatever prizes they could and leave behind no witnesses to their pillaging ways. But Doc Jennison and Jim Lane, who had been their leaders, parted ways with this disreputable bunch, for these were the dregs of the Red Legs and Bushwhackers, choosing to live a reputable life and go into politics. Now the leadership had been assumed by the bully of the bunch, Red Clark, so called because of his curly red hair, mottled complexion, and mean ways. He was the kind of man that would just as soon shoot another as to argue with him, saying it was useless to argue with stupid people. Now, having put behind them any pretense of righting the wrongs of slavery and the appearance of Red Legs, they were headed to the west, determined to keep up their ways, and as is typical for men of their ilk, they thought themselves smarter and better than other lesser men that pursued honest livings and work. They were now determined to take whatever they wanted from those that were less significant than themselves, or weaker, depending on who was making the determination. When they heard about the gold rush to Colorado, they believed that gold was calling, and they were eager to take advantage of what they thought to be a *golden* opportunity.

Dave Poole, the one everyone thought was the most dangerous, stepped closer. He was an eye-catching figure of a man, tall, slender, well dressed and groomed, always wore black with a long frock coat, tailored trousers, white linen shirt, black flat-brimmed hat, gloves, and appearing to be unarmed. But those that knew him knew he carried a Colt revolver in his belt and another at his back. Two throwing knives were sheathed at his hips, out of sight, but readily available and those were his chosen weapons, silent and deadly as he was always known to be, although usually quiet, he let his actions speak for him.

Poole stood opposite Newt and Red, hooked his thumbs in his belt and asked Red, "So, where you think we are and where are we goin'?"

Red growled as he looked up at Dave, and although he respected the man he did not fear him, and growled his answer, "We're still in Kansas an' that's the Arkansas River yonder. The trail, what some call the Santa Fe Trail, follows that river. But when it turns south, which'll be any day now, we'll keep goin' west, maybe north a mite. That should get us to the Cherry Creek gold fields in Colorado."

"And then?"

"Then we'll look things over, see what'd be the best way o' doin' things, and start workin' the claims, you know, takin' over," he cackled at what he thought was his own witty retort. "The way I see it, there should be plenty of gold for the takin', we'll just let those fools do the diggin' an' such, then we'll relieve them of the burden and 'fore you know it, we'll be ridin' high and rich!"

Poole grinned, glanced about, and said what the others were thinking, "Right now, we'd be happy with some fresh supplies, you know, like coffee an' such. There's nothing in sight and we left behind some soldier boys that weren't in too good a shape, what with bein' beat up and havin' their money taken, so I reckon the soldiers at the next fort won't be too favorable about sellin' us any supplies."

"Maybe we can find a wagon train or some settler that ain't been hit by the injuns," grumbled Red, trying to rid himself of Dave Poole, the only man in the bunch that actually made him leery and even a mite afraid, but he would not admit it. He knew

Poole was a dangerous and deadly man and one that just could not be outsmarted or outgunned. Red reached for the coffeepot, glanced to Poole, "Coffee?"

Poole grinned, turned and walked away without answering, knowing he had Red figured and knew him to be more bluff and bluster than anything. But time would tell, and Dave knew he had plenty of patience, but he could not say the same for the others. They would get to Fort Lyon tomorrow, then on to the Smoky Hill Trail into Colorado and the gold fields. Poole chuckled to himself, looking forward to Colorado and getting free of Indian country where he could rid himself of this worthless bunch of renegades. He had only stayed with them to make it this far, a man traveling alone was too easy a target for Indians. He could handle just about anything or anyone except for a raiding party of blood thirsty Indians. He had heard too many stories of the depredations of war parties and thought it much healthier to stay in a bunch, renegades themselves, but a bunch of fighters that might increase his odds of making it to Colorado Territory alive.

The bunch made short work of the bacon and the last of the venison strip steaks, the corn dodgers helped to fill the void, and the last of the coffee washed it all down. The men turned in a little early, none in the mood for small talk and with nothing to fix for breakfast, they knew they faced another day with little or nothing to eat, and worst of all, no coffee. The grumbling and complaining was soon replaced by snorts, coughing, and snoring as the bunch of misfits settled in for the night, most wondering what tomorrow had in store, but that would be another problem that would be best left until morning.

14

FORT LARNED

IT LOOKED MORE LIKE A HODGE-PODGE GATHERING OF adobe buildings rather than a military fort, but Fort Larned in its short history had already made a name for itself. With the 3rd Infantry and the 10th Cavalry, the post commander, Colonel Chester Nobles, had done an admirable job of carving out their place in the great plains, land that had been the home of the Cheyenne, Comanche, Kiowa, and Arapaho, and even after the Medicine Lodge Treaty of the previous year, those tribes were still raiding and fighting the white man at every opportunity, probably because the Peace commission had made many promises and had failed to fulfill any of them.

Cord sat on the slight bluff above the rocky abutment looking at the buildings, and based on the size and location of the different structures, he picked one of the larger ones for the commissary and sutlers post. He nudged Kwitcher off the crest of the hill and pointed the animals to the long adobe sod roofed building, bypassing the octagonal stone structure that was undoubtedly the blockhouse with the many firing ports and being the best constructed of all the buildings.

He reined up before the Sutler's building, slapped the reins around the hitchrail, and stepped into the dark interior of the building to be greeted by a whiskery faced older man with more grey than color to his beard and a dome that lacked any semblance of hair. He grinned broadly, "Howdy stranger! What can I do fer ya?" he chuckled as he leaned back on the makeshift counter that was nothing more than planks over a couple of barrels.

Cord looked about, taking in the sight and smell of the goods, leather from the harness and saddles, tart smell from the pickle barrel; stale whiskey and tobacco did not blend well with the rest but completed the experience. Cord stepped closer, "Oh, reckon I could use some .44 cartridges fer muh pistol an' rifle, and if'n you got some paper cartridges for a Sharps 50, that'd help, oh, and maybe some shells for muh 10-gauge. I'd also like some coffee and cornmeal, maybe some bacon if you got it, an' I reckon that'll do. Oh, and while you're fillin' that, I got a couple questions, if'n you don't mind."

The sutler called over his shoulder, "Go 'head on, if'n I can answer 'em, I will, but if not, mebbe I can send you to someone that can."

Cord grinned, "Been havin' any Indian trouble hereabouts?"

"Which way ya' headin'?"

"I'm scoutin' for a freighter comp'ny, one o' Butterfield's, and we're headin' on down the Santa Fe Trail to Fort Lyon, mebbe further."

"Yup, there's been some troubles. Kiowa and Cheyenne mostly, but the Arapaho have done their share too. They hit some settlers, some wagon trains, just about anything that stands still long enough. Ever since that failure of a treaty called the Medicine Lodge Treaty, and the comin' of Custer and Sheridan, there's been trouble. But Sheridan swears he'll get 'er done."

"And what about renegade white men, some callin' themselves Red Legs?"

The sutler turned and frowned at Cord, "Why you askin' 'bout them?"

"The sheriff up to Douglas County, Sam Walker, had some trouble and they left a trail of troubles headin' this way. I told him if'n I saw or heard anything, I'd send him a telegram. He says they had a reputation of hitting his town, leavin' 'fore they get caught, then comin' back when least expected, and causin' more trouble. He just wants to know which way they're headin'"

"Wal, we had a bunch come through here a while back, they was trouble alright, but din't nuthin' happen hereabouts. But I heard tell of 'em goin' down to the hog farm south of the fort and causin' lottsa trouble. Last I heard, they left one of 'em behind, couldn't get him sobered up enough to ride so they left him."

"He still there?"

"Far as I know, ain't heard nuthin' else. Lemme see, I think they said his name was Pitts, yeah, that's it, Pitts." The sutler had been busy all the while and had stacked the items on the counter and began tallying up the cost, looked at Cord and said, "That'll be four dollars 'n seventy cents."

As Cord counted out the coin, he commented, "Looks to be quite a bit'o building goin' on, they expandin'?"

"Sorta, mainly just gettin' rid of the bug infested adobe sheds, buildin' good stone structures. Got more troops comin' in to help both with the buildin' and the fightin'"

"If Major Mickey Russell, the wagonmaster with the freighters, comes in, will you let him know his scout has gone down to hog town to find out about that renegade drunk they left behind?"

"I'll do that," answered the sutler, giving Cord a glance that suggested more than he was saying that held a glint of "know-it-all" about the doin's of the young men.

Cord ignored his expression and loaded up his goods, carried them out to the pack mule and stashed them away. He stepped aboard Kwitcher and before moving out, had a good look at the fort and the many soldiers that were busy with building and more. He shook his head, glad that he had missed out on the war and the killing and more. He started south of the fort to the ramshackle buildings no more'n a mile away that made up the typical hog town where the soldiers would go to spend their meager pay and 'tie one on' before returning to duty.

————

THERE WAS no challenge to finding the man known as Pitts, as was true of most town drunks, they were the first to confront any newcomers to try to bum a drink or two. Cord had no sooner stepped down from his mount than the man tapped him on the shoulder, "Say frien', how 'bout buyin' a man a drink?" His words were slurred, his countenance mottled, his appearance dirty and smelly, his whiskers had not seen a razor in more than a month.

Cord responded, "Your name Pitts?"

The drunk staggered back, eyes wide and mouth open and drooling, "How'dju know muh name?"

"Been lookin' for you and your partners, the ones that ran off and left you."

"What'chu want wit' us? I ain't done nuthin'!" he drawled, falling back against the hitchrail, stumbling over his own feet.

"A few years back you an' your band of Red Leg renegades hit several farms near Harrisonville, Missouri, burned 'em out, killed most of 'em, and that was after the war was over," growled Cord, his anger and frustration welling up within him, but he forced himself to control his actions. The man before him was nothing but a shell of the outlaw that hit his farm.

The drunk dropped his head, drool dripping from his lip as a sob escaped. "I been fearin' this day ever since. What they done was a terrible, terrible thing. I tried to stop 'em, but they was determined to get revenge on the slave holders that they thought caused it all." He took a deep breath, tried to stand tall as he leaned against the hitchrail. "I was there, so I'm guilty too, but I wan'chu to know, I din't kill nobody, din't steal nuthin', din't burn nothin'!" The more he spoke the more he sobered, but tears began to make a trail of mud down his dirty face into his beard. He wiped his drool on the sleeve of his tattered coat. He held out his hands, "Go 'head on. Put on them shackles, I deserve it!" He leaned away from the rail, stumbled, fell to his face, and rolled to the side, dirt, and mud on his face, and he reached for Cord, but Cord moved back, shook his head, and stepped back aboard the big grulla. "Where'd the rest of 'em go?"

"They was goin' to Colorado to the gold fields. Thought them gold miner'sd be easy pickin's. I din't want nuthin' to do with any of 'em no more!"

Without another word, Cord reined the stallion around, pulled the lead taut to bring the mule, and with a wave of his hand sent Blue ahead on the trail. He needed to put some distance between him and the drunkard and the memories his presence brought. *How can a man get vengeance on a drunkard that wouldn't know what was happening or why? How can I forgive someone like that? He may not have done anything himself, but he didn't stop it either.*

He pointed the animals southwest and headed for the main road of the Santa Fe Trail. It was nearing dusk and he needed to find a campsite and have some supper. He had some thinking to do, and it probably would not hurt to try a little prayer for a change. At the mention of prayer, his mind raced back to the days with his family and listening to his Pa preach in the little country church and the times he chose to sit apart from the family and focus his attentions on the little blonde girl from down the road. He grinned to himself, picturing the girl that had captured his heart as a boy, her name was Wava Goodwin, and she was a good'un too!

15

SATANTA

DEEP IN THOUGHT, CORD RODE FURTHER THAN HE PLANNED and became aware of the lessening light as dusk gave way to darkness. He looked about, saw the thicker trees that sided a creek before him, and deeper woods to his left. He had inquired about the area and the route while at the sutler's and knew the first creek and river confluence was where Coon Creek met the Arkansas River. He chuckled to himself, nudged Kwitcher into the trees to find a clearing for a camp and with the chuckling river telling of its presence, a grassy clearing offered the temporary sanctuary he sought. He stepped down, stripped the horse and mule of their gear, and let them have a good roll in the dust and grass, then led the two to the water of the creek with Blue at his heels.

In the western sky, the half moon showed bright looking like a big white bowl rocking in the dark sky. Below the big moon, a lone bright star showed itself and Cord led the animals back into the clearing. He tethered the two within reach of the thick green grass and set about gathering some firewood to make his campfire. As he picked his way through the trees by the dim light of the moon, he stopped, bent low to look across the river where two campfires glowed. Cord went to a low crouch and moved closer, watching the shadowy figures move about the low burning fires. These were natives, looked to be a good-sized bunch, maybe thirty or more. As he watched, they finished their meal and went to their blankets, their horses picketed at the far side of the camp. Cord returned to his camp, chose to forego the fire, and dug out some jerky and used the water in his canteen to wash it down.

As he thought about the natives, he knew this bunch was probably a war party and any prey they sought would more than likely be travelers on the trail that would be followed by the freighters he was scouting for, which meant he would have to warn them. But there was the possibility the natives would stay to that side of the river, do some hunting, and return to their village. He shook his head, knowing that was probably not what they were after, and he began to make his plans for the morrow.

It was a restless night and Cord rose well before first light and was soon on the trail back toward Fort Larned. But within less than an hour, he met the freighters and the major riding out front. Cord swung his mount beside that of the major's and gave his report.

"So, 'bout how many, ya reckon?" asked the major.

"I saw 'bout thirty, but there could be more, even another camp nearby, so..." answered Cord.

The major signaled the wagons to stop, waved one of the wranglers that was tending the herd of extra mules forward and gave him instructions, "I want you to ride back to Fort Larned, tell the colonel that there's a band of injuns, numberin' over forty, that appear to be settin' up an ambush..." he paused, looked to Cord, and stuttered, "Whereabouts?"

Cord answered, "At the confluence of Coon Creek and the Arkansas."

The major looked at the wrangler, "You heard him, now git goin'!"

The wrangler nodded, swung his mount around, and took off at a run, his mount kicking up dust and dirt clods. The nearest driver saw the wrangler leave in a hurry, and hollered to the major, "What's happenin', Major?"

"Tell ya in a bit!" answered the wagonmaster and turned to Cord, "How far?"

"Half hour, maybe more."

The major nodded, "You go on ahead, if you see somethin' we need to know, don't waste anytime gettin' back hyar."

Cord nodded, dug heels into Kwitcher's ribs and with a taut lead line, the mule followed with the dog beside him, they retraced their trail of earlier but moved closer to the trees instead of in the open flats. As they neared the confluence, Cord reined up, pushed into the trees, and stepped down. Ground tying the animals, and with Blue at his side, Henry in hand, he started through the trees. Within just a few yards he stopped, dropped to one knee behind the big sycamore, and looked about. Movement in the trees showed horses legs moving surreptitiously, as he watched, he guessed there to be at least ten to fifteen, which would mean either the others had already moved through the woods or were approaching from a different direction. Cord quickly returned to his horse, swung aboard and with the mule following free-rein and the dog leading the way, they returned to the wagons to sound the warning.

When the major saw Cord coming at a run, lying low on the neck of his horse, he knew the attack was coming. He gave the pre-determined signal, and the first team and wagons swung from the trail to come to a stop crosswise of the trail, the two following wagons and team pulled up, one at the rear of the first wagon in a perpendicular formation, the second at the head of the team, also perpendicular. The following two wagons swung wide, came back alongside the second and third, making a double-stack. The last wagon closed the gap at the rear after the herd of extra animals was driven into the square. The dust had barely settled when the screaming horde of Satanta's Kiowa came storming from the trees. Apparently Satanta, realizing they had been spotted, flew into a rage, and led the charge against the freighter wagon train.

The men of the wagons, drivers, swampers, herders, and wranglers alike, all had a pre-determined position for the fight and had quickly gone to their spots. As the Kiowa horde came screaming from the trees, the men were instructed and obeyed as any well-trained army would, and being led by an experienced and bloodied major, they held fire until the major shouted, "*FIRE!*" and the bastion of teams and wagons belched lead and smoke in a roar that shook the leaves of the nearby trees.

Satanta had split his forces, spread them wide apart, and came at the wagons from the southwest and the northeast, striking at all four sides simultaneously. Had the freighters been unprepared for such an attack, it would have been a devastating and deadly assault, but the tide had been turned and the surprise was on the part of the Kiowa. The first blast from the freighters saw many of the attackers blown from the backs of their horses. But after the first cavalcade of lead, the experienced horsemen of the plains lay low on their mounts, many sliding to the offside and began firing from under the necks of the horses. But the men of the freighters showed no regard for horseflesh and the bullets dropped horse and rider time and again.

Within moments of the first assault, Satanta had

rallied his braves and retreated from the flats, disappearing into the trees. As he gathered his men around him, he made a quick review of their losses and he was determined to destroy those he saw as his enemies. He commanded his men, giving new directions and within moments the trees belched forth the rallied warriors and another devastating charge came at the wagons. Although there had been few losses on the part of the freighters, they were not the seasoned troops the major had commanded before, but they held their ground and sent another wave of death and destruction over the sage and cacti of the plains as the dust cloud of circling horses and warriors masked their targets.

And the battle raged. Although less than a half hour had passed, to the freighters it seemed much longer, but they were running low on ammunition. The major had assigned one of the swampers as the ammo carrier and he had done well, until he took a bullet through his neck. Cord saw the man fall, grabbed up the bag of ammo and quickly made the rounds, replenishing the freighters. With his Henry slung at his shoulder, he was cautious with his movements, but when a screaming warrior charged at the gap between wagons, his horse vaulting over the tongues between the double wagons, Cord dropped the bag, grabbed his Henry, and in one swift movement, took aim, dropped the hammer, and blasted the warrior from his horse, causing him to fall in a heap in the dirt. Cord moved closer, saw the bloodied side of the warrior, knew he was dead, and quickly finished the task of carrying the ammo.

Once the others were replenished, he resumed his position in the line which was at the southwest corner of the formation. Three other men were positioned, two at the back of the wagon, one underneath, and Cord took his position at the front of the wagon, behind the nervous team. Another assault came from the Kiowa, who had suffered many losses, and this was a desperate last chance at success.

The cloud of dust and gun smoke was choking, the screams and war cries of the attackers, the braying of the frightened mules, and the added stench of manure, vomit, and more was as much of an assault as the attackers. Cord coughed, spat, and took aim at a crazed warrior that was screaming his war cry and charging straight on, sitting high on his mount, a war shield on one arm, the other with a lance, and Cord dropped the hammer. The Henry bucked, roared, and spat lead and death as the bullet blossomed blood on the high chest of the man, tumbling him head over heels off his charging mount. Without a rider, the horse turned away, digging his hooves deep in the churned soil and almost falling to the side, but he righted himself and still at a run, disappeared into the dust. Cord looked about, saw another attacker swinging around the formation, lying low on the back of his horse, and with a Henry rifle like Cord's, he was firing repeatedly at the wagons, until Cord got him in his sights and ended his assault with a well-placed .44 bullet. But this wave too was stopped, and the remnant of Kiowa turned back and disappeared into the trees.

As the dust began to settle, the noise abated, and the nervous mules settled down, the major made the rounds of all the men to determine the losses. Fortunately there were only two dead, three with minor wounds, but there had been four of the mules, still harnessed in their places, that had been killed. He put the men to work, leaving half at their places in case of another attack, at the task of burying the dead and tending the wounded. One of the downed men was a teamster and he was quickly replaced by a swamper as they readied the train to move out.

With no further attack from Satanta, the major was eager to get back on the trail.

16

WET ROUTE

The sun was high in the sky when the wagons stretched out on the trail. The extra swampers rode the spare horses, carrying their rifles across the bow of their saddles, giving a show of extra guards and a readiness to fight. Cord left before the wagons were ready, to return to his duties of scouting and hunting. He followed the trail, using the rolling hills and sparse vegetation to his advantage, often riding just inside the tree line nearer the river, to travel unseen, but also giving him an advantage as a hunter looking for meat on the hoof for the wagons. He rode into the sunset, determined to make more miles and as the sun dropped below the horizon, he kept on the move, enjoying the time of day when dusk settled over the land. He wanted to ride into the darkness, knowing the moon was waxing full and he would have ample light. The horse and mule were fresh, Blue was frisky and seemed to endlessly chase any brave rabbit that dared show himself. It was the cool of the evening and the quiet of the coming night that he enjoyed most. When the cicadas, crickets, and bullfrogs at the river began to sound their chorus of the evening, he grinned, but when the coyotes began their conversations across the flats with the howls and barks that were invitations to company, he chuckled to himself and enjoyed his solitude.

It was when the constellation of Orion the great hunter, dropped near the horizon that he finally chose to stop, get something to eat and give the animals a rest. But it was shortly after first light that he was once again on the trail across the unchanging terrain. He saw a flat-topped butte set back from the river bottom and decided to take a look from on high. He nudged Kwitcher toward the rimrock butte, saw a break in the rock and a bit of a game trail to the top and dug heels to Kwitcher to make the ascent of the rather steep trail. He leaned forward onto the neck of the big horse, and the long-legged stallion dug his way to the crest.

Once atop, a quick look showed the promontory offered a great view of the outlying lands and he stepped down, retrieved his binoculars, went to the edge, and bellied down. A slow scan revealed the rolling hills, showing a buff color with dry grasses, that seemed to roll into infinity. The river made a bend to the west-northwest and could be easily seen and followed with the greenery of the many cotton-woods, sycamores, burr oak, and some hardwoods.

He saw a dim dust cloud that rolled to the south of the river, but he dismissed it as the wind kicking things up a mite.

A herd of antelope, maybe thirty or so, scampered over the distant hills and disappeared. He did a double-take at the trail in the distance, and it appeared to be a wagon train, circled and stopped, but it was so far away he was uncertain and if it was wagons, why would they be stopped at this time of day and there was something that just did not look right about the circle. He moved the field glasses across the flats, saw a couple dust devils, a group of three natives that appeared to be hunting, a lone coyote trotting across the flats looking a bit hungry as he searched for game, and nothing else that might be a danger to the freighters. He backed away from the edge, came to his knees, and started to put the field glasses into the case, when something else caught his eye. Far in the distance, the dust cloud seemed to be moving nearer and the size of the cloud was growing. He turned back, went to one knee, and lifted the binoculars. As he focused in on the base of the dust clouds, a slow grin split his face for he was looking at a massive herd of buffalo, rumbling this way, and would probably reach the river well before dusk.

Cord rose, returned to the animals, and replaced the field glasses into the case and into the saddlebags. As he swung aboard, he was thinking about the buffalo, and knew he better use the Sharps, and there would be no need to take more than two, at most three. That would be a lot of meat and Cooky would have to dry some for it to keep, but the men would enjoy the change of pace at dinner, and they had been known to put away a goodly amount of meat at each and every meal. And although Cord had never eaten buffalo before, he had heard it was a tasty meat and he looked forward to the feast it would provide. He nudged Kwitcher to the narrow trail that split the rimrock and started off the butte.

The Arkansas River took a slow turn from south and slightly west to basically west. The big bend in the river covered about fifteen miles, and the low water in the wide river offered a good crossing for the massive herd. The dust cloud followed the herd on a straight run toward the bend in the river. Although Cord's experience with bison was nil, he assumed they would be crossing for the herd was moving at a quick walk and covered ground without any hinderance sufficient to slow their progress. He tethered the animals in the thicket of sycamore and with Blue at his heels, he moved to the edge of the trees, picking a position still within the trees, but offering a clear field of fire at whatever target he chose on this side of the herd.

He had chosen a huge burr oak that stood close to a hundred feet tall and had a trunk that had to be close to ten feet in diameter. He was not about to take any chances trying to gain cover behind some scrawny cottonwood or lesser tree, knowing the monstrous bison, especially in a herd on the move, could level any smaller tree. As he leaned against the big oak that he called a mossycup oak, the leaders of the herd, a couple big cows splashed into the water, and as the herd slowed for the crossing where the water was shallow and the sand bars wide, the dust cloud moved with the slight breeze and overtook the leaders. Cord planned to use the oak as a leaning rest, stabilizing his shot, until the corner of his eye caught movement off to his right. He turned his head slightly, scanned the flats and saw a band of natives, mounted, and lining out to await the herd. Beyond them in the flats, a convoy of followers with travois laden with hide lodges, some leading the horse with the travois, others riding the animals, but many were walking. He had hung the binoculars at his neck and lifted them for a better look at the procession and saw the families and others, knowing this entire band was a hunting party. He turned to look on this side of what would be the route of the herd and saw another band of mounted hunters that had taken position in the wide dry wash, masking their presence from the herd.

Now Cord had a decision to make, should he take a buffalo or retreat into the trees and leave the herd to the natives. He shook his head, his decision made for him as he spotted the first of the herd cows coming from the water, closely followed by what he guessed to be several hundred if not a thousand or more pushing the leaders onward. He let much of the herd pass, watching and learning as several herd bulls moved at the edges of the herd as if in a protective position, guarding the more vulnerable of the herd, the cows with calves. As they passed, Cord was able to distinguish the bulls, and especially the young bulls. That would be his choice, pick a couple, maybe three young bulls, drop them as close in as possible, and leave the herd to the rest of the hunters.

He saw a pair of young bulls splashing through the water and waited for them to crest the bank, as they came in line, Cord dropped the hammer on the first bull, saw it stumble, drive its chin into the dirt in a slide to its chest and belly. Cord had quickly opened the breech, slipped another cartridge into the breech, and brought the lever closed. He took a quick aim at the second bull that saw the first bull drop, and the second took a quick sidestep to avoid the downed bull, moved past the downed bull, and Cord squeezed the trigger on the big Sharps. Again the shot was on target, just behind the front leg, low in the chest, and the bull dropped his head, driving his big dome into the dirt and flipping over on his back, probably breaking his neck in the tumble. Cord did not move, but reloaded and picked a third target, a young cow without a calf. He squeezed off his shot and dropped the third beast. He was surprised that the roar of the Sharps was drowned out in the drumming of the hooves that seemed to shake the ground, and even the loud blast of the Sharps was not loud enough to startle the beasts.

As Cord lowered the rifle, he grabbed at his neck-erchief and slipped it up over his nose and mouth, already he had begun coughing in the dust that reeked of the stench of urine, feces, sweat, and more that was carried by the massive herd. Cord dropped to one knee, reloaded the rifle, but sat it down butt first at his side as he continued to watch the amazing sight before him. Although the dust rode with the herd, he could see them stretch out to the north for a distance he guessed was a half mile, probably further, for he could no longer see the leaders of the bison herd.

It was well past mid-day and into the afternoon when the last of the herd passed Cord's oak. He had gone into the trees to retrieve the horse and mule and led them from the woods toward the downed carcasses of the three buffalo. Although he had stretched out well ahead of the freight wagons, he was kind of hoping they would show up and give him a hand with dressing out the kills. He ground tied the animals, slipped the Sharps back into its scabbard, and as an afterthought, slipped the Henry out and leaned it against his first kill. He stood looking at the big beast, shook his head, and slipped the Bowie from the sheath and began his work of splitting it from tail to nose, and once he had the entrails out, he would cut off the head, legs from the knees down, and begin skinning the carcass. He stood up, looked down at the beast, and shook his head at his foolishness of killing three.

Blue suddenly came to his feet, stepping away from the gut pile and letting a low growl give warning to his master. Cord slowly turned, shaded his eyes to see three riders, all natives, coming near. They stopped, looking at Cord and the three downed bison, and one of the three nudged his mount closer.

He growled at Cord, "Why are you here?"

Cord nodded, let a grin cross his face, "I'm scouting and hunting for a wagon train of freighters that's coming behind me. This is for them."

"Who are you? What are you called?" asked the man.

Cord had noted the lack of war paint, but two of the horses had been marked with painted designs that appeared to be about hunting. He looked at the man, "I am called Cord. My full name is Cordell Beckett. What is your name and who are your people?" he asked, motioning to the talker.

"I am Walks with the Wind. My people are the To-kinah-yup of the Ka'igwu; your people call us Kiowa."

The three men wore similar attire, fringed buckskin leggings, breech cloths, fringed buckskin tunics with the fringe dyed a deep red. They wore their long hair in braids that held different decorations, some with colored rabbit fur, others with material or beaded bands. Their hair was pulled back from the faces, broad foreheads, narrow eyes, stoic expressions, and red porcupine tufts that held at least one feather. They were a noble looking trio, none showing interest or friendliness.

"Walks with the Wind, I am honored to meet you. I have taken three buffalo, and I would like for your people to take those two." He grinned, motioned to the downed bull he had been working on, "That's a bit more work than I expected, and I won't get them," motioning to the other two kills, "finished, and I don't want them wasted. You would do me an honor if you would take them."

Walks turned to the others, spoke in his language as the others, obviously angry and making less than friendly gestures, prompting Cord to step closer to his Henry and loosen his duster to give access to his pistol. He watched as the others argued, then Walks with the Wind waved the others away, and turned back to face Cord. "We will accept the gift of the two buffalo. The others went to get some of the women to come and do the cutting of the bison. I will go now," he paused, looked down at Cord, chuckled, "I saw you go to your weapon, that was a good thing to do. You are welcome in our land at any time. Tell any of our people that Walks in the Wind has said it is to be so, and it will be so."

"Thank you, Walks in the Wind. You are a good man."

Walks frowned, nodded, and reined his mount away and left, head held high and his rifle across his legs. Cord let out a breath he did not realize he had been holding and relaxed, returned to his task. He was about half way through the skinning of the beast when a small group of women with a couple children came toward him, leading two horses with empty travois. One woman that Cord thought to be quite pretty, came near, motioned to his bull, and said, "Work of women. We will finish for you," and waved him away as if dismissing him from their presence.

Cord chuckled, grinning, and with a shrug, started to his mount and the woman said, "Leave the mule. We will load," and turned to the work without another look at Cord.

17

MOON

Dusk was settling across the land when the women motioned Cord back to the butchering site. They had finished with his bull and had moved on to the others. The meat had been deboned and stacked on the hide that lay flesh side up. Cord quickly loaded the panniers and more with the cut meat, took a couple parfleches that were normally a part of the mule's load, placed them behind the cantle of his saddle and strapped the more of the meat atop the panniers. The mule was loaded to capacity and there was still some meat left on the hide. Cord looked to the busy women at the next carcass, walked to them and did his best to explain he could not carry it all and they were to take the rest and the hide. The one woman who did the talking nodded her understanding, gave Cord a broad smile, and turned back to his work.

As he rode from the scene of the great hunt, a

backward glance showed several butchering sites where campfires had been lit, and some of the men were already enjoying the fresh meat for their supper. The flat was freckled with fires and Cord was surprised to see even more on the far side of the kill site, where another group of hunters had also made a kill. But he turned back to the trail and pushed on, knowing it would be after dark before he made it to the wagons, but he needed to lighten the load on the mule before he could stop for the night.

"Wal, I was wonderin' if'n you mighta run into some buffler! What with the big dust cloud we saw, we figgered that's what it was!" declared Cooky as Cord rode into their camp. Cooky had already fed the men, and a few were still sitting around the campfire as Cord stepped down and walked back to the mule. He began stripping off the load, passing it to Cooky and his helper and a couple of the men who volunteered to help.

"Say, this is right fine meat. You done good, Cord, an' these fellers are gonna be eatin' mighty fine for a couple days. You could prob'ly e'en take a day off! Hehehehe," cackled Cooky, glancing to the few men still at the campfire. Cooky looked at Cord, "Say, how 'bout you? You et yet, or mebbe you need some good stiff coffee?"

"I could use some coffee," answered Cord, looking about. "Major around?"

"Yup, he's o'er yonder by that there water wagon. He usually spreads his blankets some'eres about."

Cord accepted the big cup of steaming black coffee and started toward the camp of the major. When he stepped into the light of the small fire where the major sat with another of the teamsters, he nodded to the major and asked, "Got a minute, Major?"

"Wal, h'lo, Cord, sure, sure, sit down!" he answered, motioning to a stool near the fire.

Cord took his seat, waited while the major finished his instructions to the teamster and turned to him. "So, how's things goin' on the scout? Anything I should know?"

Cord grinned, sipped the coffee and leaned back against the sideboard of the wagon and explained, "Well, I brought in some fresh buffalo for Cooky, and he was pleased. But I met up with some natives, good bunch of 'em too. They was friendly 'nuff, I gave 'em a couple kills and that pleased 'em. But as I was leavin', I noticed what appeared to be the camp of another bunch on the far side of where the buffalo passed. Looked to be a mite bigger'n the one I met up with, figgerin' five or six to a fire, there would easily be another fifty, sixty more natives."

"Those that you dealt with, what kind?"

"Kiowa, I believe."

"Hmmm, well that other camp could be more of them, or maybe Comanche. Sometimes those two tribes fight each other, sometimes get together to fight the army or make raids on wagons an' such," explained the major. "Either way, it don't bode well for us." He lifted his own cup and stared into the flames of the fire, slowly shook his head, looked up at Cord and added, "Tell you what, you go on scoutin' and you'll probably come across that other band, but you be careful and stay out of sight if you can, and if there's somethin' about that bunch or the first ones too, that you think I need to know, you hustle on back here and let me know."

"Alright Major, but if I can't come back, I'll do my best to leave you a message the same way I leave sign for hangin' meat, alright?"

The major nodded, "That'd be fine. I'll tell the men to keep a sharp lookout and keep their weapons near, just in case."

Cord nodded, tossed the dregs of his coffee aside, and returned to leave the cup with Cooky and mounted up to find himself a solitary camp, there were too many people here.

———

THE SUN HAD YET to show its face when Cord rode from his camp in the trees. The first light of early morning cast a dim shadow before him as he nudged Kwitcher to the trail back to the site of the buffalo hunt. The passing of the massive herd had made the flats north of their crossing look more like the fresh plowed ground of an eastern farmer, but this was a wide swath of turned ground, and Cord chuckled as he thought of the many farmers that would plow the land, plant the seed, fertilize it, and work in many ways to bring forth a crop, and this passing herd had plowed and fertilized it in one move. He pushed across the swath of land, watching for sign of any of the natives and the only sign of those he had met, showed the band had moved north, maybe to follow the herd.

Just beyond the strip of churned soil, Cord came to the sign of the other native hunters. He stepped down to get a better look at the tracks, noticing the sign of passing horses, walking moccasin clad people, travois and more. But this group was moving south to the river. He paused, looked about, stood and pushed the hat back on his head as he scratched at his thick locks, and squinted at he looked and thought. He walked across the trail, leading his animals and with Blue at his side, and at the edge of the trail, he saw older sign that showed when they had originally come north with the herd. He thought *so they came north for the hunt, and now goin' back south. Must be a totally different band, but wait...* He went to one knee, examining the sign. Something was different, then he realized the group going north with the herd was much larger, and now those going south were about half the number. He stood again, slowly shaking his head, trying to resolve the questions that were circling in his mind.

"Those are the tracks of the *Yaparuhka,* Comanche," came a voice from behind him. Cord did not move but casually dropped his right hand inside the flap of his duster to rest on the butt of his pistol and slowly turned to face the voice. He grinned as he saw the young woman who had sent him away from the buffalo as they finished the butchering. He thought she was pretty then, but now in the rising light of early morning, she was beautiful. She sat aboard a white horse that showed no other color, a rarity. She wore a beaded buckskin tunic over fringed leggings. Her hair hung in braids that had been braided with tufts of dyed orange rabbit fur, and her smile added light to the morning.

Cord relaxed, looked around for others but there were no others, and he smiled, "You speak English very well. Where did you learn?"

"As a child from the black robes that came into our village." She leaned on the pommel of her carved rawhide and bone saddle, and added, "Those," motioning to the tracks—"are the Comanche women and children. The men have gone to the hills to fight. They are led by *Quenatosavit,* White Eagle. They are angered because the white men have not honored the treaty of Medicine Lodge and they have turned back to the way of war."

Cord stepped closer, "Why do you tell me this?"

"You were kind to us. You gave us buffalo to feed my people. They," nodding toward the way of the tracks that led north—"wait for your wagons to come. They will take the wagons, kill everyone."

"How do you know this?" asked Cord.

"That is the way of White Eagle. He believes he

and his people have been wronged and the white man did not speak the truth when they had the treaty for them to make their mark."

"What about your people? The Kiowa?"

"They have also been lied to by the white soldiers, but they have taken the women and the buffalo back to our village. Our chief, *Ton-a-en-ko,* Kicking Eagle, will lead our people when they join with *Mah-vip-pah,* Wolf's Sleeve, the chief of the Apache, and they will also go against the white soldiers and others."

Cord, stepping closer still, looked at the woman, "Is it safe for you to tell me this?"

"No one will know, but you were kind, and it is the way of my people to be kind to you as well."

"I am called Cord, what is your name?"

"I am *Öakar kaaywich*, Yellow Singing Bird," she answered with a smile.

"Do you have a family? You know, a man, children."

She smiled, "I know family. And no, I have no man. Do you have a woman?"

"No," he chuckled, grinning and motioned to his animals, "All I have is a horse, a mule, and a dog."

Yellow Singing Bird swung down and stepped beside Cord as he turned to walk with the sun at his back. She smiled and stepped out with him. Cord looked at her, "I'll be going to Fort Dodge today. I'm sure you know where that is, don't you?"

"It is one day's ride," she said, nodding to the west-northwest. "If you like, I will ride with you."

"I'd like that," responded Cord, glancing to the woman. "Won't you have someone wondering where you are and come looking?"

"They know I am out hunting; they will not know I have gone."

"Gone?"

"I choose to leave the Kiowa people. I was traded to them by the Comanche. The Comanche took me from my people when I was very young, my people are the Caputa Ute of the distant mountains. I must find my way back to my people."

Cord frowned, looked at the woman, slowly shaking his head, "Taken and traded? It must have been a long time ago, I thought you were a Kiowa and you worked with them."

"I have been with them for five summers, but I am not one of them. They see me as a captive, a slave. It is not good, and I have wanted to leave since I was traded, but could not. That is why I want to go with you."

"I don't know if I can get you all the way back to the land of your people, but while you are with me, you will be safe," assured Cord, uncertain of what he would do with her. Yet he knew he could not send her back and would not take her with him to the wagon train, but for some reason he felt obligated to her and his concern for her safety was heavy on his mind. He sighed heavily, slowly shook his head and said, "Well, we have a ways to go. Might as well ride!" He jammed his boot in the stirrup and swung aboard. He watched Bird as she grabbed the pommel of her saddle and swung aboard without using a stirrup and landed astraddle of the tall white horse and looked to Cord with a broad smile.

18

FORT DODGE

FORT DODGE STOOD LONELY ON THE PRAIRIE, LYING TO THE lee side of a low bluff on the north, the meandering Arkansas River well south and the stone and wood buildings, although new within the past two years, appeared as if they had been there for many years. Cord was sided by Yellow Singing Bird as they rode into the complex of buildings. Laid out in a square with the parade ground and the ever-present flag-pole in the center, Cord guessed the long building with several men standing at the hitchrail was the sutler store and from the looks of it, probably the saloon also. Beyond the store, on a bit of a rise, appeared another line of buildings that Cord guessed to be the headquarters and officers' quarters. With a nod to the curious men, Cord and Walks continued on toward the headquarters building.

He was confronted out front by a man with

stripes on his sleeves, "An' what be your bizness hyar?" growled the crusty sergeant.

"I got somethin' to report to the commander, concerning the Comanche," answered Cord as he leaned on his pommel, one arm over the other as he glared at the sergeant.

"Wait there," he growled and cast a sidelong glare at the woman, mumbling something as he turned. He stepped into the building, returned soon, and said, "The colonel will see ya now, but not her!"

Cord looked at Bird, "Will you wait?"

Bird smiled, "Yes, I will wait."

Cord stepped down, followed the sergeant into the headquarters and was ushered into the main office where an officer sat behind a desk stacked with papers. He looked up at Cord, growled, "What is it?"

"Well, Colonel, back at the bend, I ran into a big herd of buffalo and a band of Kiowa hunters. We shared some meat and I left, but returned early this morning and met with a woman who helped the night before. She said the other bunch of hunters were Comanche led by a man name of *Quenatosavit*, White Eagle. She said they were plannin' on hittin' the soldiers and any travelers cuz they were plumb mad at the whites not keeping the treaty of Medicine Lodge."

The colonel paid attention when the name of the chief was spoken, leaned back at looked with a frown at this man before him that looked a little trail worn. "What were you doin' there?"

"I'm scoutin' and huntin' for a train of freighters comin' this way."

"You say she's Kiowa?"

Cord nodded, "No, she's Caputa Ute, taken captive by the Comanch and traded to the Kiowa. Been with 'em for 'bout five years and she said their band is not too happy either and she suspected they too would do a little fighting."

"Why she tellin' you all this?"

"I helped them out with a couple buffalo, and she was grateful."

"So she says; you can't trust any of 'em."

"Well Colonel, you do with it as you will. I did what I needed to do by tellin' you, now it's up to you," growled Cord, turning back to the door.

"Just a minute!" mumbled the colonel, "Let me show you somethin'." He stood, walked around his desk, and said, "Follow me," and Cord obliged. Once outside, the colonel led the way around the building and stood at the corner. With a glance to Cord, he lifted his hand and pointed to the hill above and beyond the fort, "See that camp up there? That's General Phil Sheridan, he and his bunch, with more comin', think they're goin' to finish this Indian problem, as he puts it, in short order. He's got Colonel Custer comin' with a couple companies of cavalry and they're gonna solve all our problems, or so he thinks. So, I'll have one o' my junior officers take your tale of woe up to him and he can do with it whatever he will." The colonel harrumphed, kicked at a rock, and turned and disappeared back into his office.

Cord slowly turned, glared at the back of the officer and without another word, turned back to the hitchrail where Bird awaited, still sitting astride her horse. Cord and Bird had rode from the parade ground, reined around the corner of the sutler's store, tied the animals off at the hitchrail and started into the store but were stopped by a sharp remark from one of the loafers outside.

"What'chu doin' with a squaw? Cain't you find yo'sef a real woman?" called out a man that obviously had too much to drink, and his remark prompted the laughter and catcalls from the others.

Cord stopped, turned to face the men, and moved Bird behind him. He took one step toward the man and in a low voice said, "My father taught me to never give any attention to fools and drunks, and since you qualify on both counts, I will heed my father."

He glared at the man who frowned, coughed, and looked at his friends who were waiting for his response. He looked at Cord, "You cain't talk to me like that!" he declared and started a roundhouse swing toward Cord's head. Cord leaned back just enough so the man's fist caught nothing but air, while Cord's boot heel stomped on the man's foot, brought his knee up to meet the man's face as he bent toward his hurting foot, then Cord doffed his hat and repeatedly slapped the man with his hat, dust flying everywhere. Both he and his cohorts were caught by surprise and none of the others moved as the man slumped to the ground at Cord's feet, coughing and spitting and moaning. Cord looked at the others, "Anybody else?"

The men stood silent, glancing from Cord to their friend, and one shook his head, "Nope. You said enough, an' he was wrong."

Cord nodded, turned back to Bird, and both entered the sutlers. While they were inside, Cord heard the crusty sergeant barking orders at the men to return to their barracks with because they were movin' out in the morning to meet a wagon train of freighters. He ended with, "We're leavin' at first light!"

———

CORD LOOKED across the campfire at the woman as she prepared the two rabbits on a spit to cook over the fire. She had fetched them while Cord tended to the animals when they were making their camp in the trees by the river. Cord had prepared the coffee and sat back to wait for the coffee dance to begin and enjoyed watching Bird busy at her preparations. He chuckled to himself thinking *I could get to likin' this, but the last thing I need is to drag along a woman.*

He rose from his seat, walked to the stack of gear, and rolled out his blankets. He knew she had a bedroll behind her saddle, and he rolled it out on the far side of the fire, his actions noticed by Bird, but she continued with her cooking. Cord walked to the horses and mule, Blue at his heels, and checked their pickets, keeping the white mare well away from Kwitcher who had already been sniffing around the newcomer and was well aware of the mare, but she was not in season, so Cord was not concerned.

Bird had dished up their supper on the plates, handed one to Cord, and took her own and sat on the log beside Cord. They ate in silence for a while until Cord asked, "Yellow Singing Bird, how'd you get that name?"

She smiled, took a sip of hot coffee, and looked at Cord, "When I was young, before I was stolen, I could mimic the songs of most of the birds. I made the call of the Meadowlark more often because I loved the song. My people do not give names to the young ones until something tells them the name. I was called Wanderer before that because I would go to the woods alone. But the last thing I remember from my mother was when she said I was just like the Yellow Singing Bird, and she said that would be a good name for me." She dropped her eyes and ate a little more, looking at Cord, "The name you call your horse is a strange name, why?"

"Oh, you mean Kwitcher?"

Bird nodded, sipping on the last of her coffee.

Cord chuckled, "When he was young and I was breaking him, he was a mite disagreeable, so I would say, 'Kwitcher bitin', Kwitcher kickin', Kwitcher buckin',and it took a while to get him to settle down. But I realized I was sayin' Kwitcher all the time, so...it stuck!"

Bird snickered and smiled at Cord. "And you are called Cord, like a rope or a string?"

"No, Cord is short for Cordell. It was my grandfather's name and my mom thought it a good one, so, I'm Cordell, or Cord."

Bird dropped her eyes and said, "You lay my blankets away from yours, you do not want me near?"

Cord chuckled, "Oh, I do, but it is not proper for us to be together like that because you are not my wife. You see, my father was a preacher, a man of God, and he was firm in his beliefs and what the Bible, God's Word, says about such things. That was one of his messages that kinda stuck so, I reckon it best we don't share the blankets."

"Do you have one of those books with God's Word?" asked Bird, her curiosity rising.

"Yes, there's one in my saddlebags, but I haven't used it in some time."

"Why?"

Cord sighed heavily, looked at Bird, "Well, it's like this. My pa always taught about how God would take care of us and such, but when a band of outlaw renegade Red Legs hit our home, killed my family, burned our home and such, I just had a hard time believing what my pa used to preach. I've been on the trail of that bunch since I became a man, figger on evenin' the score a mite, get some justice." He paused, took another deep breath, glanced to Bird, and added, "Maybe I'm wrong, but I already caught up with one of 'em, an' he was a worthless drunken' sot, so I let him be, guess I forgave him of what he done, but I ain't too anxious to be forgivin' of the others."

"Would you tell me of the things in God's Word?"

"Mebbe, but not tonight. Let's get us some sleep so we can be on the trail by first light."

Bird smiled, nodded, and rose to go to her blankets. Cord watched and was aware of the beauty and grace of the young woman.

19

COMANCHE

As Cord led the way from the camp, he heard what he first thought to be distant thunder and stood in his stirrups to look all around in the dim light of early morning. Although there was heavy cloud cover, there was no lightning and the typical rolling sound of thunder was not there. What he heard was more of an intermittent rattle that faded away and returned on the wind. There was a lull in the sound as the wind began to pick up and a dust devil danced across the flats before them. A long-eared jackrabbit bounced from under a sage and was chased by a scrawny-looking coyote, but the fast maneuvering rabbit soon lost the hungry canine.

Cord looked at Bird, "I'm thinkin' that was gunfire, and if it was, that ain't good!"

Bird just glanced to Cord, looked down the trail but the rolling hills offered little in the way of a long-distance view. The Arkansas River lay to their left and the Santa Fe Trail lay north of the river, usually about fifty to a hundred yards and while the river meandered, the trail held steady and straight, at least as much as the terrain would allow. With the sun slowly rising behind them, Cord kept a sharp eye to the east, the direction that was the source of the gunfire. They traveled west, staying on the trail until that uneasy feeling that caused hair to rise on the back of his neck, prompted Cord to nudge Kwitcher off the trail and take to a lone rise that appeared to parallel the trail and lay about a hundred yards to the north.

As they crested the rise, Cord, with a quick look about, nudged Kwitcher over the crest, then turned back to the west, staying just below the rise. They made another three or four miles before the sight of thin wisps of smoke filled Cord with caution. As the rolling hills offered a bit of a swale and just beyond a rise with a higher crest that might give him enough of a promontory for a better look, a glance to Bird as he pointed with his chin to the hill and nudged Kwitcher that direction. As they dropped into the little swale, Cord reined up and stepped down, ground tied the mule and stallion, watched as Bird picketed the mare, and Cord started up the hill. With his Henry hanging at this shoulder by the sling, he carried the binoculars and dropped into a crouch as he neared the crest. He went to his knees, crawled to the crest, and bellied down.

He lifted the binoculars and scanned the source of the smoke, all the while gritting his teeth as he watched. What had been a wagon train of at least twenty wagons, was now a circle of black as the smoldering ruins gasped the last bit of smoke from the fires. All around the scene, warriors were digging through the rubble, most of the bounty already piled off to the side, but they still searched for anything that was missed during the fight. Cord saw the remains of several of the settlers tied to the wagon wheels, the burned bodies hardly recognizable as human. The many horses from the wagons had been rounded up and herded into the center of the circle while the warriors finished their pillaging. It was then that Cord noticed several white women in tattered clothing that sat in a group near the horse herd, watched over by several braves.

"They will be taken back to the village and made into slaves, if they live that long," came the soft voice of Bird who lay beside him. He had not moved, nor had he heard her come close, but it was that sensing that told him she was near.

"What will they do to them?"

"They will use them as they please, torture them if they do not cooperate, kill them. But there is nothing you can do, there are too many warriors. They are Kiowa and Comanche."

"Both Kiowa and Comanche? I thought they were enemies?" asked Cord, still watching the plundering below.

"Yes, but they fight together against the common enemy, the white man."

As Cord watched, he counted the women, and saw two warriors grab one, lift her to her feet and take her beyond the herd of horses, out of sight. The other women, young and old, huddled together until a group of warriors came at them, grabbing them and pulling them to their feet. One grabbed a white-haired woman who stumbled, jerked her upright before him, pulled her back against him, and slit her throat, dropping her to the ground, writhing and kicking.

Cord gritted his teeth as he lowered the binoculars, letting Bird take them and he turned away, shook his head, and fought with himself about trying to rescue the women. But his mind wrestled with his heart, and he knew it would be a foolish stunt, for there were probably over a hundred, maybe as many as two hundred warriors, and one man could do nothing but sacrifice himself at the altar of foolishness and good intentions. Bird rolled to her side, handed the binoculars back to Cord, and said, "They are leaving, there are no women with them."

"You think there are any survivors?"

"No."

"What will they do?" pointing with his chin to the different bands of warriors, one going north into the hills, the other crossing the river to the south.

"Return to their villages, until the next time they need to kill."

"So, with the freighters coming along the trail after us, you think they will be safe?"

"I do not know. Sometimes they leave a scout to tell of what happens or if there is any other prize to be taken."

———

As they rode up to the remains of the wagon train, Cord noted there were no bodies of warriors any where abouts, and Bird noticed him looking around and said, "They always take their dead with them. Different people have different ways to honor the dead, some are buried, some are put in caves, others are put high up in trees or on scaffolding for the dead in a place for their dead."

Cord nodded and said, "They have great respect for their dead, but none for that of their enemies."

"Because they believe in an afterlife when their enemies could come against them again, so they try to destroy the bodies so that will not happen."

Cord wanted to make a cursory examination of the battle scene, just to know for himself what happened and if there was anything he might do. There were too many bodies, some burnt to ashes, others just burned beyond recognition, and some that lay sprawled about with signs of mutilation and desecration. The stench of death was on the wind and carrion eaters were already showing themselves scurrying about the scene. Both women and men were mutilated, and even the children. Cord had been too young for the war and had not seen such horror before and his stomach churned as he gagged at the scene. He leaned to the side and left his breakfast behind, wiped his mouth with his neckerchief, dug heels to Kwitcher, and rode from the spectacle.

Cord rode in silence, replaying the scenes of death as he allowed his mind to revisit the horror. The stench of burned flesh, puke, and other human waste, as well as the smoke and ash seemed to follow them on the wind, but nothing could take the smells from them. They put a good five or six miles behind them as the trail and river bent to meet one another. Cord moved into the trees, motioned for Bird to step down, as he tethered Kwitcher and the mule. When Bird did the same, they walked together to the river and Cord spotted a backwater pool that was just what he wanted. He looked at Bird, "I need to get that stench out of my nostrils and clothes. I'm gonna go for a swim, how 'bout you?" he asked, slipping off the duster and hanging his pistol belt and pistol from a nearby branch.

Bird smiled and started to slip her tunic over her head but was stopped when Cord spoke up, "Whoa! Whoa! Not yet!" He chuckled and motioned, "I don't mean together, one of us has to keep watch what with that attack on the wagons, there could be any number of Kiowa, Comanche, and renegades movin' about just anywhere." He pointed to the bend of the river where a backwater pool pushed against the overhanging grassy bank, "You get your washin' done there, and I'll be settin' up camp and keepin' watch till you're done, then we'll trade off. Maybe by that time I'll have the cookfire goin' and you can take over and maybe do some cookin', 'sides, your cookin' is a whole lot better'n mine!"

Bird laughed, grabbed up a blanket to use as a towel, dug out her spare tunic and more, then laughing all the way, walked back to the deep water. A glance over her shoulder showed Cord had already taken the animals to the small clearing in the thicket of trees and was not watching her. She smiled and quickly stripped off and splashed into the water.

Cord laughed to himself as he started gathering the firewood, remembering her expression and laughter when he stopped her from stripping down. He knew that modesty was not a common thing among most natives, and it was nothing for men and women to bathe together, but he wasn't quite ready for that, maybe his father's teaching was a little more ingrained in him that he realized. He thought she would go in, clothes and all, as he was about to do, but when she started to strip, he had to stop her.

He had the fire going, the coffee pot filled with fresh water, and the pans laid out beside the back-strap off the deer he had taken earlier, when Bird came walking into the clearing, drying her hair with the blanket and smiling broadly as she looked pret-tier than a brand new copper penny. He grinned, chuckled, and said, "So, now it's my turn. The

Henry," he pointed to the rifle leaning against the grey log set back from the fire, "is loaded and ready if you need it."

She smiled and nodded as they passed one another, bumping into him intentionally but appearing to be accidental, and as he turned, she tossed him the big bar of lye soap, smiling broadly as she did. Cord chuckled, walked on, anxious to rid himself of the stench of death and more. As he waded in, he began scrubbing the clothes with the bar of soap, first the duster, stripped it off, rinsed it out, wrung it out and tossed it on the grass. Then his shirt, his britches, and finally the union suit. While he was busy with his laundry, Bird was busy preparing the meal and Blue lay at her feet. The two had become best friends and he seemed to prefer her company to Cord's.

Cord shook his head as he waded from the water, went to his packs to get a blanket to dry off, then dug through the gear for clean dry clothes and when fully dressed, joined Bird at the cookfire. She pointed to the coffeepot for him to put the coffee grounds into the water and he complied, sat back on the log, and watched her at work. She was efficient in all that she did, no wasted motions, no uncertainty, always confident and smiling. She looked at him, smiled, and said, "I found some raspberries and more. We'll have them for our desert, if you like."

20

CIMARRON

THEY RODE FROM THE TREES AS THE RISING SUN BENT ITS first rays over the eastern horizon. The low rolling hills showed as nothing more than a shadowy line of darkness at their backs and the western sky was doing its best to keep the last bright star from snuffing out its lantern, but the darkness retreated, slipping below the western hills before them. Cord stood in his stirrups, looking all about, seeing the cloudless sky arching overhead, and said, "Looks like another beautiful day!"

"Every day is a beautiful day when you have rested, eaten, and enjoy those you are with," declared a smiling Bird.

Cord dropped into his saddle as they topped a slight rise. The river lay off their left shoulder and the rolling land often hid low swales, dry gulches, grassy flats, any of which could hide an abundance of game or danger. Before they crested the slight rise, Cord heard movement that sounded like several creatures running through the deep grass. He grabbed his Henry from the scabbard under his right leg, jacked a round into the chamber, and nudged Kwitcher over the crest.

A small herd of antelope were moving quickly through the grasses, heading for the river for their morning water and Cord and Bird were spotted as they showed themselves over the crest of the little knoll. But Cord was quick to bring the Henry to bear, picked a young buck and snapped off the shot. The Henry barked and the buck fell, but Cord frowned when he saw another buck stumble and fall. He quickly looked about to see if there were other hunters, but there was no one. He glanced to Bird who sat smiling, her bow in hand as she leaned on the pommel of her saddle. "Did you shoot that second buck?" asked an incredulous Cord, looking at the grinning girl.

She laughed, "Why are you surprised? I have often hunted and taken game with my bow."

"Yeah, but..." stammered Cord, frowning.

"But what? Why is it so hard to believe? Sometimes it is better to take your game without all the noise of your rifle."

Cord just shook his head as he replaced his rifle in the scabbard and nudged Kwitcher to the first downed buck. He glanced to Bird, "I'll get started on this one, you can do that one."

"Do not cut the hide. It makes a very soft leather," ordered Bird, giggling and smiling.

———

By late morning, the two rode into the Ranch at Cimarron Crossing, into what appeared to be a massive fort that rose up from the ground in the middle of nothing but grass and cactus. Set on a slight rise above and north of the river, the structure looked to be almost a hundred yards square with a wide double gate on the north side, offset from the round tower with gun ports that stood guard over the kaavl or central grounds and the land to the north and east, on the opposite corner stood another tower that covered the south and west. As they entered the structure, to their right was the stables that stretched almost the length of the north wall, and matching corrals and stables on the south wall, but on their left was the main building that housed the owners and the store.

Several wagons, both freighters and Conestoga and prairie schooner types, were parked about the exterior walls and men were busy all about the compound. Cord and Bird reined up at the hitchrail by the main building and Bird waited, while Cord entered the store.

He was greeted by a jovial figure with a handlebar moustache that drooped over the corners of his mouth, "Howdy friend! Welcome to the Ranch at Cimarron Crossing. Lookin' for supplies?"

"Yessir," answered Cord, "and to share some information and hopefully leave some meat for a train of freighters that's followin'."

"Well, let's start with the supplies, oh, and I'm Bob Wright," he motioned to another man that was busy stacking some goods on shelves—"and my partner there is A.J., A.J. Anthony." He extended his hand as he spoke, showing what Cord assumed was a grin under the whiskers.

Cord extended his hand to shake, "And I'm Cordell Beckett, I'm scoutin' for the freighters that'll be along, probably later today. One of Butterfield's trains and ramrodded by Major Mickey Russell, and here's a list of supplies," he offered as he extended the scrap of paper.

"Good, good," stated Wright, handing the list to his partner, A.J. "And what was the information?"

"There was a wagon train wiped out 'tween here and Dodge, and from what we could tell it was a combined party of Kiowa and Comanche. No survivors, everything burned."

"How'd you know there were no survivors and why do you think it was both Kiowa and Comanche?"

"Well, we got there right after the fight while they were still strippin' things, watched 'em with my binoculars as they left. Then we went down among 'em. And we know they were Kiowa and Comanche because the woman out there," nodding to the door —"was a captive of the Comanche, lived with 'em a spell 'fore she was traded to the Kiowa. So, she knows."

The man stepped to the window to look out at Bird, looked back at Cord, "What're you doin' with her?"

"Takin' her back to her people, the Caputa Ute in Colorado."

"How many warriors were there?" asked the cowed clerk, almost afraid to look at Cord and speaking softly.

"Oh, 'tween one an' two hundred I reckon."

Wright lifted his head, raised his voice to his partner, Anthony, "I told you! Didn't I tell you!" he barked, shaking his fist. "We need to close up and git!" Wright looked at Cord, "We've been hit too many times, lost some men the last time, and it's just not worth it! And on top of it all, even when we had help the last time, they turned out to be as bad as the Indians!"

Cord frowned, "Whaddaya mean?"

"Oh we had a bunch of outlaws in here, said they used to be Red Legs but were goin' to the gold fields. Needed some supplies and when it came time to pay up, the just started loading up, but the Indians attacked and they helped fight 'em off, so we let 'em go without payin', not that we coulda done nothin' about it anyway, they was seven of the meanest lookin' outlaws you ever did see, and most of our men were out in the grass cuttin' it for the stables! Tweren't nuthin' me'n A.J. could do against all them!" He looked to his partner, helped stack the order on the counter before Cord, then looked at Cord, "Is that all?"

"Yes, that's all the supplies I need, but..." He paused, pointing to the rack behind the counter, "Can I look at that Henry?"

Wright grabbed the Henry rifle from the rack, handed it to Cord and explained as he watched as Cord worked the action, looked down the muzzle, and held the rifle to his shoulder. "That was taken as part payment from another wagon train, it's got a few scars, but appears to be in good working order."

"Got a scabbard for it?"

"Sure, sure," answered Wright, reaching under the counter for the leather scabbard and lying it on the counter before him.

"I'll take the rifle and the scabbard and throw in four boxes of shells also," stated Cord. Wright smiled, did as asked, then tallied up the order, showed Cord the numbers and as Cord counted out the money, he asked, "And would it be alright if I left a couple skinned out antelope for the freighters when they come?"

"Sure, hang 'em in this end of the stables, they'll be safe there, but be sure to cover 'em with some sacking or somethin' to keep the flies off'n 'em."

———

WHEN THEY RODE from the Ranch at Cimarron, Bird was smiling and fingering the stock on the Henry rifle that was stuffed into the scabbard under the right stirrup. She looked at Cord, "Why did you get me a rifle? I've never shot a rifle before."

Cord chuckled, "I'll teach you about using that, but I got it because we're travelin' alone and there's a lot of unfriendly folks out here in the middle of nowhere and it would be better for both of us to have a rifle, just in case we need the extra firepower." He grinned, and added, "Besides, you *can* use that for hunting also, you know."

They had ridden about another seven or eight miles when they came to what most would call a point of rocks that stood a lonely sentinel rising up from the low rolling hills and standing strong with its crown of rocks, here in the middle of dry land that had little else than cactus, coyotes, and sage. But it beckoned the travelers and Cord looked at it as they approached, thinking *God musta had an extra handful of rocks and just dropped 'em right there.* He shook his head, grinning at himself as he realized he was talking like his pa most always did, referring to God as if He was standing right there next to him.

Cord looked at Bird, "Let's make camp there in the trees by the river, opposite those rocks."

Bird nodded, and nudged the white mare that direction, and with a glance to the sun that was doing its best to paint the western sky in shades of orange and red, "There's time for you to get us fresh meat for our meal." She laughed at Cord as he looked back at her.

"Anything special you have in mind?"

"I saw some prairie chickens that would taste good, or maybe some ducks ..." She shrugged and smiled.

Cord thought to himself, *Hmmm, reckon I got my orders, better not disappoint.*

21

VISITORS

❋

F ROM THE C IMARRON R ANCH WEST TO THE P OINT OF Rocks where they made their camp, the trail left behind the more fertile grassy plains and began to show more sage, cacti, creosote brush, scraggly piñon trees, and little else besides the often seen dust devils kicked up by the occasional breeze that crossed the prairie. This was dry land they traveled through and little settlement, nothing like the many farms that were cropping up across the grassy flats, this was more desolate and lonely. Although they cut sign of wagon trains, the occasional stagecoach stop, and stragglers from the buffalo herds, Cord and Bird seemed to be all alone.

But about a dozen miles after the Arkansas River bent to the southwest, about the time the day was getting short and everyone was a mite tired, Cord reined up and nodded ahead. Thin wisps of smoke lazily trailed upward and disappeared into the hard blue sky. Although the sun was threatening to set and they were wanting to get a good campsite near the river, he said, "Let's take a look yonder, some-thin' don't feel right," and he nudged Kwitcher forward. He leaned back and slipped the Henry from the scabbard, jacked a round into the chamber, lowered the hammer and lay the rifle across the pommel of his saddle. Bird followed suit.

As they neared what they now recognized as a burnt barn that had not been much before the fire, it was nothing but burnt timbers and stacks of sod now. The stench of burnt flesh hung in the air, and Cord spotted the remains of a burnt carcass that bore some resemblance to a milk cow. As they neared what had been the sodbusters dugout, he saw where two bodies had been spread-eagled and mutilated, before a fire had been built on the forms. It was obvious one was a man, the other a woman. Cord lifted his neckerchief over his nose and mouth and saw Blue trotting to a mound behind the soddy. Cord and Bird followed and saw Blue duck out of sight on the far side and let a bit of a bark, more like a cough, escape. Cord stepped down, rifle in hand and followed the dog as he dropped into the smashed in entry to a root cellar. Cord grabbed the broken boards, cast them aside and stepped into the dark interior. It had been ransacked, but Blue was scratching at the broken shelf before him.

"What're you doin' boy? There ain't nuthin' there," explained Cord, giving a low whistle to call the dog back. Blue reluctantly obeyed, but whimpered as he moved, looking back at the broken shelves. Cord thought he heard another low whistle, frowned, and turned around to see if Bird was making the sound, but she was not in sight from the interior of the root cellar. Again Blue whimpered, and trotted back to the shelf, scratching against the back wall. Cord, frowning, sat the rifle down, pulled away the remains of the shelf and saw a leather drawstring hanging from a small hole in the boards covering the back wall. He moved the remains of the shelf, saw what appeared to be a door hung on leather straps, and pulled the draw string, drew the door open, to see the figures of two huddled children, wide-eyed, shivering, holding tightly to one another, and scared to death.

One started to whimper and the other pulled closer. Cord said, "It's alright, I'm friendly. Come on out, we'll see some daylight. It's alright, c'mon." He spoke softly, smiling, and reaching out a hand but the youngsters pulled back. Cord dropped to one knee, "I'm not going to hurt you, and whoever did all this is long gone. C'mon now, let's go get you cleaned up and get you something to eat, alright?"

As the two youngsters stood together, Cord saw a boy and a girl, both about the same height and probably close to the same age, he guessed maybe ten or twelve, but he was no judge of children. Cord smiled, dropped to one knee with an arm over the shoulder of Blue, "I'm Cord and this is Blue," He pulled Blue close and rubbed behind his ears. "C'mon out, we'll get you some food." He motioned the two youngsters toward him and the steps leading from the root cellar where dim light seemed almost blinding. The two shaded their eyes, still holding tight to one another, and took tentative steps to the entryway. As they climbed from the cellar, Cord and Blue followed and Cord called ahead, "Bird, they're comin' out. Step on down and make 'em welcome."

As the two stepped into the light, Bird dropped to one knee with her arms held wide and a broad smile on her face, "Hello you two. We're your friends and we'll take care of you now."

"Where's our pa an' ma?" whimpered the boy, still holding the girl close as he looked around in the dim light. "What'd they do to the house," he paused, looking about, "an' the barn?"

He stumbled as he started to walk toward the house, but Bird reached her arm around them, and the boy stammered, "Pa? Ma?" he tried to call out, but the girl was holding on to the rags of his clothes so tight, he could hardly move. The boy looked at Bird, "Hey, yore a injun!" he declared.

"Yes, but I'm not of those who did this to your home. I was a captive and Cord freed me and now he's taking me back to my people. Do you have any family that live nearby?" she asked, slowly standing and resting her hand on the boy's shoulder.

"Why? Where's Pa?" asked the boy, a little louder as if calling for his father.

Cord came alongside and asked, "Do you know who did this?" nodding toward the burnt remains of the farm.

"Pa said he thought they were Comanche. He saw 'em 'fore they got here and tol' Ma to take us to the cellar, but she left to go back with Pa."

"How long you been in there?"

"Ma put us in there 'fore we had breakfast. It's a secret room Pa made to hide out."

"What's your names?" asked Bird.

The boy looked at her, glanced to his sister, "She's Trish, I'm Trey. We're twins."

Blue had pushed his way between the young-sters, and both petted the friendly mutt as they walked, Cord on one side, Bird on the other as they led the animals behind. As they walked past the ruins of the house and the bodies of the parents, Bird did her best to shield the children from the view, but they were determined to look, and Trish put her hand to her mouth and stifled a cry as she leaned against Blue and reached out a hand for her brother. Cord hustled them on and away from the scene as quickly as possible. He spoke up, "I caught a glimpse of a break in the trees near the river, thought we'd head thataway and make camp, get a fire goin', cook some food, get some rest. Whaddaya say kids? Hungry?"

Trey glanced to his sister, looked at Cord, "Yeah, we're hungry. Ain't had nuthin' to eat since last night." His response was little more than a mumble, but Cord understood. This was probably the worst day in the children's lives and at their age, it would be hard to try to understand and Trey was reminded of his own loss, when the Red Legs had hit his farm and murdered his parents, burnt everything before leaving him with nothing but a pile of ashes and bitter memories. He shook his head as he thought about it, looked to the youngsters, and knew they were quite a few years younger than he was when he lost his folks, and this would be hard. He looked at Bird, knew she too had suffered similar losses, and shook his head at the way of things, and with a glance to the night sky he mumbled to himself, "*Why God, why?*"

As they made camp, Bird sent Cord and Trey to the river with a Cord's fishing gear, which was nothing more than a ball of string, a couple hooks, and the shovel to dig some worms. Cord grinned, nodded and put his arm on Trey's shoulder and said, "Looks like us men got to get some fish for supper. You a good fisherman, Trey?"

The boy grinned, nodded and with a stoic expression, answered, "Tolerable, just tolerable."

Cord chuckled, "Well, we're gonna hafta be better'n tolerable if we wanna eat, ya reckon?"

Trey just nodded and grunted his agreement as he walked beside Cord. They cut some willows, dug some worms, and were soon sitting side by side on the riverbank, letting the bait drift with the current into the deep water at the bend. Cord let the moment be savored by the boy for a short while before asking, "You have any family nearby?"

"Uhnuhn. Ain't got none. Pa allus said he was a only child an' Ma lost her sister when she was little. They said our fam'ly din't move out here till after the war. Said they lost all their family in the war." He picked at a tuft of grass, slipped a long piece in his mouth, and chewed; he was choking back his sobs and started to lower his head, his shoulders shaking.

Cord rested his hand on the boy's back, "I know how you feel, Trey, it's alright, let it out."

Trey turned suddenly, glared at Cord, "How do you know how I feel? They din't kill your folks an' burn yore farm!" he growled, shaking his head, and driving his fist into the grass at his side.

"Yes, I do know how you feel. I had the same thing happen to me," answered Cord, speaking softly and slowly, his words filled with memories and understanding.

Trey frowned, wiped the tears from his eyes and turned to look at Cord. "It did?"

"Ummhmm, but it was outlaws that killed my family and burnt my farm."

"Oh," came a soft reply from Trey as he turned back to watch his line. He suddenly grabbed at his pole, jerked it back and set about landing a nice trout. He had no sooner taken it off the hook than another one bit Cord's line and the two fishermen were suddenly busy landing a mess of nice trout for their supper.

The fishermen were more jovial as they worked at cleaning the fish and hanging them on a forked stick to carry the big batch back to camp. As they walked into the clearing they were greeted by the two females with a "Where you been? We've been waitin' for our supper!" declared Bird, glancing with a smile to Trish who stood beside her, both with their hands on their hips and looking at the two.

And they indeed had been busy, the coffee had perked, and the pot now sat on the flat rock beside the fire, the frying pan was ready with grease already sizzling, and the cornmeal was on a plate awaiting the fish. Trish rolled the fish in the cornmeal, handed them to Bird and they soon had a panful of frying trout and more waiting. As they came from the fire, Bird dished them up to the children first, then to Cord and one in her own plate, reloaded the skillet and after passing around some biscuits and dishing up some fried Indian potatoes, they set about devouring the meal.

They set out at first light with the slow rising sun at their backs. Trey rode behind Cord and Trish behind Bird. They were a bit of an odd looking family, Cord, dark-eyed, thick whiskers, heavy brow, and dark hair, the two youngsters with reddish blonde hair, fair complexions, freckles, and blue eyes, and Bird with her dusky complexion, black, shiny hair, dark eyes that danced with light all the while, and her trim figure in the buckskin tunic and fringed leggings; they were an odd looking family alright.

But they were learning much about one another and growing closer with every mile and every day. There was nothing but uncertainty ahead and nothing but bad memories behind, but it was a good land before them and mountain ranges of high country beckoned and they were making time to the west.

For the next four days, the travel had become routine with Cord taking game for meat for the freighters, yet never staying still long enough for the wagons to catch up to them, although he would often lag behind a little until he saw the wagons coming, then he would pick up the pace and make time. The only settlement they passed were the few stage stations of the Barlow & Sanderson Overland Mail Company, and the few stage stops that had a semblance of a trading post attached, usually to make a little extra money for the station keepers. It was at the second station after the youngsters joined them that Cord stopped and traded for a couple more horses, both young geldings and because they were only about fourteen hands, they were not the first pick for any other horse traders, but they were just the right size for the twins. And with a couple saddles thrown in, the family group was all mounted and made a little better time.

On the eve of the fifth day after the foundlings joined them, they sat on a bit of a knoll looking down at the meandering Arkansas River and the post known as Fort Lyon. Cord knew they were in Colorado Territory now, and this fort was the last of the line for the freighters and this would be the parting of the ways from the freighters. They made camp in the trees near the river, knowing the wagons would not be along for at least another full day, and with fresh back strap venison steaks sizzling over the fire, they gathered around the campfire to enjoy the time together.

"What do ya suppose is gonna happen to us now?" asked Trey, staring at the fire, and giving a sidelong glance to Cord.

Cord lifted his eyes to the boy, glanced to Trish and Bird and tossed a twig into the fire and drawled, "That's a mighty big question, Trey. I've been thinkin' about that and y'know, I just don't have a good answer for you. And not just you, but all of us. I've been on the trail after the outlaws that killed my family, and the last I heard about them, they were headed up the Smoky Hill Trail headin' to the high country. And Bird there, she's been wantin' to get back to her family, the Caputa Ute people that also live in some of the high country out west, but neither one of us want to let you two go anywhere without us, so...I guess I just don't quite know how to answer that question just yet, but...I'm workin' on it."

22

REVELATION

CORD LEFT BIRD WITH THE YOUNGSTERS AS HE RODE INTO Fort Lyon to meet with the commandant and learn about Indian activity in the state. He noticed a wagon train of settlers camped outside the fort and nodded to one of the lookouts as he rode past and into the central compound of the fort. When he stepped down at the headquarters building, he noticed little activity within and even the sutler was not busy. Cord stepped into the sutler's building, looked around and the sutler, standing behind a counter with his arms crossed over his canvas apron, asked, "What can I do you fer?"

Cord sauntered near, "Not much activity for a fort for this time of day. Somethin' goin' on?"

"Nah, it's Sunday and the chaplain is out to that wagon train and they're gonna have 'em a combined service. And what with all them settler types and their women folk, it gives these sojer boys a chance to smell perfume instead of sweat an' horse manure! Heheheh." He cackled as he looked to the door and beyond. He pulled out a briar pipe, stuffed it full as Cord stepped a little closer. The sutler lit his pipe, exhaled a cloud of smoke and with the pipe firmly in his teeth, said, "Need sumpin'?"

"Yeah, I got me a list here and got a couple questions," Cord was sifting through a pile of what appeared to be children's clothing, glanced up to the sutler, "I'm surprised to find kid's clothes in a store for the soldiers," and chuckled as he picked out a few items.

"Wal, we git settlers in here ever so often, some of 'em trade goods like that, but most need things after the long journey. Not too many, mind you, but some," explained the sutler, beginning to fill the list given him by Cord.

Cord glanced at the man as he busied himself, "Any injun trouble hereabouts recently?"

"Nah, not too much. After Chivington done his best to kill all of 'em, both Arapaho an' Cheyenne, they ain't bothered us too much."

Cord frowned, "Chivington?"

"Yeah, ain'tchu heard 'bout that?"

"Uh, no, can't say as I have."

"No matter, it was just a time when one o' them officers, Chivington the name, who led his sojers agin a village of peaceful Cheyenne, Arapaho an' a few Cheyenne. Kilt 'em all, men, women, chilluns, or most of 'em anyhow. Big stink 'bout it too, but ain't nuthin' gonna happen."

Cord shook his head, thinking about all the desolation he had seen, both that done by natives and that done by white men, soldiers, and outlaws both. *A lot of wrong done by both sides, red and white. Reckon evil isn't confined to any one race, no matter the color.* He looked up at the sutler, "Have you heard anything about some Red Legs, Bushwhackers, comin' out this way, causin' trouble?"

The sutler paused, looked at Cord, "Friends o' your'n?"

"No, but a sheriff back in Kansas asked me to keep a lookout for 'em. Said they been hittin' places around his town, then leavin' and comin' back a month or two later and doin' it all again. He just wanted to know if they were headin' back his direction."

"Wal, I don' know if'n it was the same bunch, but I heard tell about a band of what they called rebel guerrillas hit a couple places, kilt 'em all, burnt everthin', tried to make it look like injuns but they din't fool nobody. A neighbor saw 'em leavin' and said they was all white men, scruffy lookin' bunch too."

"How long back?" asked Cord.

"Oh, lemme see now, I reckon it'd be at least a month, prob'ly longer."

Cord settled up, packed up, and left the sutler's

to return to their camp. As he swung aboard, he noticed several of the soldiers walking from the fort toward the settler's wagons, and as he passed the wagons, he saw the folks were setting up the chairs, benches, and blankets to get ready for the service with the post chaplain and the preacher with the wagons. Folks were settling into the chairs and more, visiting with one another and Cord looked to the trees where the camp was and nudged Kwitcher to a bit of a trot, pulling the lead line to the mule taut. He was swinging down when he heard the music start back at the wagons and Bird and the youngsters had walked to the edge of the trees to look that direction.

She looked at him as he stepped down, "What's the singing about?"

"Oh, they're havin' a get together for a church service, you know, singing, preaching from the Bible, that sort o' thing."

"Could we go?" asked Trish, looking up at Bird and over to Cord. "We used to go to church all the time 'fore we came west and stopped at most towns to go to church. It'd be nice to go if it's alright?" she pleaded, looking with wide eyes at Cord.

Cord chuckled, glanced to the same expression on Bird and Trey, and nodded, "Oh, I suppose it'd be alright. But you think you might wanna put on these new clothes 'fore ya' go?"

"New clothes?" declared the children in unison as they came near to accept the packages, smiling broadly, and hurrying into the bushes to change.

Cord looked at Bird, smiled and said, "Let me strip the horse an' mule and we'll go, or better yet, how 'bout you three startin' out and I'll catch up? Oh, and better take a blanket to sit on."

He chuckled as Bird snatched up a blanket and as the youngsters came from the bushes, wide smiles painting their faces as they looked down at their new clothes, trotted to the side of Bird and she, with one child in each hand, started to the circle of wagons. Before they got there, Cord caught up and with Bird at his side, pushed into the circle, saw a likely spot to sit, and spread the blanket. The people were standing and singing the song, "He Leadeth Me."

> *He leadeth me, O blessed thought!*
> *O words with heav'nly comfort fraught!*
> *Whate'er I do, where'er I be,*
> *Still tis God's hand that leadeth me.*
> *He leadeth me, He leadeth me,*
> *By His own hand He leadeth me,*
> *His faithful foll'wer I would be*
> *For by His hand He leadeth me.*

The handful of musicians included a man on a guitar, one on a banjo, a woman with a zither on her lap, a young man with a concertina, and one with a Jew's Harp. But they made good music, and everyone was enjoying themselves. The preacher stepped behind the makeshift pulpit, a tall upright wooden box, and with a broad grin, complimented the people on their singing, then added, "There's a new song that is simple and has a good message. For those that don't know it, listen close and you'll catch on real quick. It's called 'Jesus Loves Me.'" He stepped back and the zither started it off, the rest joining, and the people began to sing...

Jesus love me! This I know,
For the Bible tells me so;
Little ones to Him belong;
They are weak, but He is strong.
Yes, Jesus loves me!
Yes, Jesus loves me!
Yes Jesus loves me!
The Bible tells me so.
Jesus love me! This I know,
As He loved so long ago,
Taking children on His knee,
Saying, "Let them come to me."
Yes, Jesus loves me!
Yes, Jesus loves me!
Yes Jesus loves me!
The Bible tells me so.

The Army chaplain stepped forward, lifted his hand high to motion the people to be seated and as they were settled, he began, "It's a joy to have so many here this morning. We don't often get to enjoy a service like this, especially with so many lovely ladies. There is a Bible character named Jeremiah, he was referred to as a voice crying in the wilderness, so it is appropriate that the preacher this morning is also named Jeremiah." He turned to face the man seated behind him and motioned him forward, looked to the crowd, "Ladies and gentlemen, Pastor Jeremiah Winslow!" Everyone stood, applauded, and were quickly seated at the motion from the pastor. He smiled broadly, opened his big black Bible on the pulpit and looked at the crowd and began, "I'd like to take my text from Hebrews 13:5-6 *Let your conversation be without covetousness; and be content with such things as ye have: for he hath said, I will never leave thee, nor forsake thee. So that we may boldly say, The Lord is my helper, and I will not fear what man shall do unto me.*

"We've just come through a terrible time in our country. A civil war when many people suffered great losses. Some lost everything, like one man that was a neighbor who lost his family, his home, everything! And he stood looking at Heaven, mad at God and shook his fist at God and asked, 'Why? Why God' and stood there hopeless and heartbroken, thinking all was lost and indeed he had lost much, but he was alive, and he had tomorrow just over the horizon, and whether he knew it or not, he had God right there by his side." The pastor paused, looking around at the many upturned faces, seeing heartbreak in the eyes of many, questions in the eyes of others and more. He continued, "And at a time when so many have suffered great loss and wondered why, or like that of the man I spoke of, it is easy to get mad at

God, shake your fist, fuss at Him, turn your back and more. But you're not the only one that suffered loss, think about it, God's only son Jesus, was taken by a crowd, mocked, beaten, and hung on a cross, who *died* on the cross, shed his blood for all of mankind and gave his life for others. But God willingly allowed that to happen. Oh, He could have stopped it of course, but if He did where would we be? We would be on our way to Hell forever!" he proclaimed with a loud voice and slamming his fist on the pulpit.

He stood quiet, looking at everyone before him, and in a calm and quiet voice, he continued, "Our text tells us God never leaves us nor forsakes us. Even in our darkest moments, and when we feel all alone, when we don't understand, He's still there. But what do we want? That's the covetousness that our text tells about—covetousness is that earnest desire for something we don't have, maybe something of others, and we really want it instead of what we have, and God says we are to live a life without that covetousness and that we are to be content with such things as we have. How many times have you seen something that belonged to someone else and thought, 'I'd like to have that!' That's what He's talking about, when you get your eyes off the things, life, situation, whatever that others have, and realize that God is by your side, you can say *The Lord is my helper, and I will not fear what man shall do unto me.*

"We all know what fear is, we've lived through a terrible war, and we've traveled across some desolate country just to get this far. We've been confronted with restless natives, outlaws, weather, hard places and times, and yet, here we are! Now it's time to look forward, put our hand in God's hand, and go with the confidence He is right beside us. Let's put the bad time behind us and step out with God. Oh, but wait, some of you have never accepted the promise of God and received Christ as your Savior. Let me ask you, if you were to die today, do you know for sure that Heaven is your home? Do you? If not, you can be sure, because God is with us today and He extends His hand of invitation to you, each and every one, young, old, in-between, and that invitation is to receive that free gift of eternal life and take Him as your savior and secure your place in Heaven today. Won't you do that?"

Bird turned and looked at Cord, "Is that true, what he says? You know, about the gift of eternal life and having Him as your Savior?"

Cord dropped his eyes, took a deep breath as his mind and thoughts flashed back to the times he sat and listened to his father preach the same things, and looked at Bird, slowly nodding, "Yes, it is. It's the most important thing to know."

Bird saw some people getting to their feet and walking forward to the makeshift altar where the pastor and the chaplain waited, and she looked at Cord. "Have you done that? Accept Him as savior?"

"Yes."

"Should I go with them?" nodding to the others going forward.

"If you want to accept Christ as your Savior, yes. And...I'll go with you."

Bird smiled and started to rise but felt a tug on her tunic, looked down to see Trish with tear filled eyes as she asked Bird, "Can I go too?"

At the same time, Trey touched Cord's hand and looked up at him, "What about me? Can I come too?"

Both Bird and Cord nodded, stood, and with each one holding onto the others, they walked forward to talk with the pastor. The preacher was standing, saw the small group coming, and stepped out to greet them, "So, would all of you like to accept Christ as your Savior and make sure of Heaven?"

Cord answered, "I've done that pastor, but I've been one of those that have been a little mad at God, but I want to get that right, and Yellow Singing Bird and Trey and Trish would like to receive Christ as Savior."

"Wonderful, wonderful. Now let's join hands..." He began to explain about sin, and it's penalty of death, and how Christ paid that penalty and purchased each of us a gift of salvation that all we have to do is believe with all our heart and accept that gift by prayer. When he asked if they understood, each one nodded and he said, "Now, let's pray together. I'll lead, and you can repeat those words, but only if you really believe, alright?"

He looked at each one, saw heads nodding, and

he began to pray the simple prayer of acceptance of the gift of salvation paid for by Jesus on the cross. When he said "Amen," each of the others did also and they had a group hug to celebrate. Then the pastor added, "We're having a dinner for one and all, and afterward, we'll have a baptismal service this afternoon, you're welcome to join us!"

23

MOUNTAINS

"Say, mister! Kin we jaw wit you a minit?" Cord was walking back to his camp when he encountered the couple, who hurried along to catch up with him. Cord saw a scruffy-looking man, whiskery face but no beard, tobacco-stained teeth, dirty and ragged clothes, and wild eyes under a floppy, raggedy hat. The woman was much the same, so skinny her face looked skeletal, bad teeth, scared eyes, and dirty hair stuffed under a tied up scarf. Her clothes were just as dirty and ragged as the man, and her toes showed through one of her shoes. Cord smelled them before he saw them, but he stopped and turned to face the pair.

"Say, we noticed yo' fam'ly," he chuckled as he glanced from Cord to his woman and back, "an' those kids don' look like they're your'n. So, we was wonderin', are they waifs 'er sumpin'?"

"Why?"

"Wal, we noticed you had'ju a squaw woman, and since them kids ain't hers and don' look like your'n, we wondered if'n you wanted to get shut of 'em."

Cord frowned, "Why?"

"Wal, we be gonna settle out'chere, you know, build us a house, put in a farm, and doin' all that takes a lotta work. Now we got us one young'un, but he ain't 'nuff, so we thot mebbe we'd take them two off'n yore han's and have a couple more workers for the farm, you know."

Cord turned on his heel, growling as he did, and started to leave but the man grabbed at his arm to stop him, "Now wait a minit," he pleaded.

Cord jerked his arm free, stood spread-legged, gritting his teeth, and with eyes squinted he did his best to control his contempt and growled, "Don't ever put your hands on me, and don't ever think I'd let even a porcupine or a skunk into your hands, much less two innocent kids! You lazy lout! Get outta my sight 'fore I do somethin' we'll both regret!

"Wal, I never..." whined the man, his woman holding on to his arm, as they watched Cord disappear into the trees.

———

THE PATCHWORK FAMILY rode from the trees and kept to the trail that sided the Arkansas River, heading west. In the distance, the faint shadowy western horizon showed as a jagged line of shadows, made so by the distant mountains, the first time seen by Cord and the youngsters. Bird smiled, "It has been many summers since I saw the mountains. When we get closer, we'll probably see snow on the higher peaks."

"Snow? It's summertime! There won't be snow, surely not," stated Cord, frowning as he looked at Bird who rode beside Trish. Trey was to Cord's right, Bird behind Cord and Trish behind Trey and all could hear what Bird said.

Bird smiled, "You'll see. I remember places where the snow never left the high country all summer long."

"So, that don't look so far. Reckon we'll make it by dark?" asked Cord, glancing to Bird.

Bird smiled, slowly shook her head, "Maybe in three days."

"Three days? It can't be that far!" declared Cord, looking from Bird to the horizon and back.

Bird just smiled and rode silently, with an occasional glance to Trish and Trey, and the glimmer of mischief and affection in her eyes as she watched the continual moves of Cord's hips as he rocked with the cadence of Kwitcher.

Since he left Missouri, he had continually queried from those that might know anything about the western lands, and when they were readying to leave from Fort Lyon, he spent time with the freighters wagonmaster, Major Russell, who had made several trips to the west beyond Fort Lyon and like most explorers and adventurers, he had harbored the information of the land and the people in his mind. When Cord explained his mission, the major understood and gave him several cautions, about both the land and the outlaws. "It's a growing country, growing faster than any law and men make their own way. When someone does something that would usually be handled by a lawman, the people have to take care of it themselves. And usually, the good people keep things in check, sometimes by holding their own court and carrying out their own sentences, but I reckon that's the way it's always been done. Most folks know that if they want a good life and to live in peace, they have to take a stand against evil. I read in a newspaper about a man name of John Stuart Mill who said something like, 'Bad men need nothing more to compass their ends, than that good men should look on and do nothing.' So, I think you're doing the right thing, but here's some things you need to know..." and he continued to give Cord more detail about the trails leading into the mountains and the gold fields and what little he knew about any law. "They've formed an outfit called the Colorado Rangers, kinda like the Texas Rangers, but..." he shrugged. "I think you'll be on your own, so watch your back."

Based on what the major had explained, Cord knew they would follow the Arkansas River and in three to four days they would come to El Pueblo. "But if'n I were you, what with travelin' with that

there Ute woman, you might wanna be a mite careful. Although it was a long time, maybe fifteen years,
ago that the Ute and Jicarilla Apache attacked there
long about Christmas time, and kilt near ever'body.
Some folks still remember that and might be a little
skittish, but...it's been a long while, so mebbe..." he
shrugged. "Then after that, it's another day or two to
Cañon City, it's kind of a supply center for the gold
country up in South Park. Or...you could keep
followin' the river west to Cleora. There's a stage
road that goes through the canyon, and it's about
three days to Cleora. From there, you go north to
California Gulch, another three, four days. That's
another gold town."

They rode the edge of the slight bluff above the
meandering river bed that carried the Arkansas
River. The many bends offered sandy banks, gravel
bottom riverbed, and scattered cottonwoods, burr
oak, silver leaf maple, and berry bushes galore. They
stopped for nooning, and the youngsters reveled in
picking the many berries, although most were yet to
ripen, they still gathered a good lot and everyone
enjoyed the change of pace. As the youngsters frol-
icked in the shallows of the river, pulling up their
britches and skirt to wade in the cold water, Bird
looked at Cord, "What are we going to do with those
two?"

Cord chuckled, "If I knowed that, we'd a done it
already. But I keep rememberin' what muh pa used
to always say, 'The Lord works His work in His own

time. We get too impatient and want to do things our ownselves, but His time is always the best.'" Cord chuckled, "And I would get so exasperated at him sometimes, I was not a patient youngster. I wanted everything right now, no waiting, and it took me a while to learn to wait on God, but Pa was right, His timing is best."

The terrain showed little change, flat land prairie with sage, buffalo grass, greasewood, with an abundance and variety of cacti and the ever-present whirling dust devils. Dry country with the only green showing along the banks of the Arkansas River, their choice for campsites where there was grass for the animals, water for all, and occasionally a fishing hole for some trout. They circumvented El Pueblo, with no need for supplies and ample time they chose to take a round about way south of the town, but on the north bank of the river. After a week of travel, they were nearing the mountains, or at least the foothills of the higher mountains, but even the foothills were bigger than anything seen by Cord or the youngsters. But the most prominent and picturesque of the entire mountain range, stood just to the north, the tall peak with granite shoulders and whose crest rose so high above the rest it appeared to scratch the blue of the sky above.

Bird watched as Cord and the youngsters stared at the big peak, and she said, "My people call it *Tava* or Sun Mountain. The Arapaho call it *Heeyotoyoo* or Long Mountain. It has been said that the early explorers that wore the metal armor called it El Capitán."

"I see what you mean about the mountains having snow. That is snow up there, isn't it?" asked Cord, nodding to the peak that stood head and shoulders above the surrounding hills.

"Yes, but there are many more mountains, even bigger and with much more snow," she nodded to the west. If we go further into the high country, you will see many such mountains."

"The major said this next town is called Cañon City, and we'll stop there, pick up a few supplies, visit with some folks, find out more about the country."

"You wish to find out about the men you hunt?" asked Bird.

Cord frowned, "How'd you know about that?"

Bird smiled, "I listen, you talk, others say what you want to hear."

"Those men you look for, they the ones that killed your family?" asked Trey.

"That's right, Trey, but they did more than that. They left a trail of dead bodies all across this country and they need to be stopped."

24

CAÑON CITY

<small>As they rode into Cañon City, they caught the eye of</small> many of those that were bustling about on the boardwalks. Although the town was not especially busy, the small group that included two youngsters and a native woman was not the usual sight on the street of this bustling little town. Although some of the buildings showed vacant, most were occupied, and several were busy with wagons out front and people moving about. Cord reined up in front of a mercantile, a two-story stone building that stood across the street from a similar building that had a sign saying Baldwin House, apparently a hotel or boarding house. With the horses tethered at the hitchrail, everyone stepped down and filed into the mercantile, the youngsters staying close to Bird as they looked wide-eyed at everything about. Shelves were loaded with canned goods and other items,

racks behind the counter held rifles and shotguns, a display counter showed an assortment of pistols, and open barrels held pickles, flour, sugar and more. Cord walked to the counter where a matronly woman stood with a broad smile splitting her face as she greeted them, "Well, hello folks. How can I help you?" as she looked from Cord to Bird and the children.

Cord stepped close, "Well, we could use some clothes for the youngsters, and I have a list of supplies we need," he began as he lay the list on the counter between them. The woman picked it up, looked it over and said, "Ummhmm, I think we can fill this. I'll get started while you and the missus look around."

Bird walked to a table that had children's clothes stacked about and began looking at the different items, Trey and Trish standing beside her and watching, sometimes fingering the fabric of some, while across the table from the three another woman, auburn hair, with a girl a little younger than Trish but with a big smile and reddish-blonde hair, did much the same on the far side. But children did as children are wont to do and moved closer as Trish began talking to the girl, "Hi, I'm Trish, what's your name?"

"I'm Amelia, but most call me Amy." The little girl looked from Trish to Trey and then to Bird and, with a nod to Bird, asked Trish "Is she your mother?"

Trish smiled, glanced to Trey, "For now."

Amy asked, "There's a swing out back, wanna come?"

Trish looked from Amy to Bird, "Can we?" she asked.

Bird glanced to Cord, back to the children and said, "Yes, for a while, but don't go anywhere else."

The three trotted off and out the front door, turning to the side to make their way around back of the store to the swing and more. It was a bit of a playground with a teeter totter, two swings, and a knotted rope swing. Bird followed the youngsters, and the mother of Amy soon joined them as they watched over the children. The mother of Amy came near, as both women watched the children playing together, and she asked Bird, "Are you watching over the children for their mother?"

Bird glanced to the woman who appeared friendly enough and answered, "No, their parents were killed by some raiding Comanche. We found them in a root cellar. They said they have no other family."

"Oh my, how terrible, the poor dears. But they seem to be doing well. The man inside, he your husband?"

Bird smiled, but did not answer, just kept watching the children enjoying the swing and talking with the other girl.

The woman glanced to Bird, "I'm sorry, my name is Beatrice, and you are?" she asked, extending her hand, and painting a smile on her face.

Bird looked at the woman, paused a moment and answered, "I am Yellow Singing Bird of the Caputa Ute people. My friend, Cord, is taking me home to my people. I was taken from them when I was about the age of your child," she said, nodding to the happy-go-lucky girl that was swinging high after being pushed repeatedly by Trey.

"But, but, if you go to your people, then what about the children?" asked Beatrice, somewhat stunned at the thought of white children being taken to a native village.

"Cord says that God will show the way and the time."

"Oh," declared Beatrice, surprised at the mention of God. "Then he is a Christian?"

"We all," nodding toward the children— "accepted the gift of salvation and were baptized, but Cord had already done that before."

"Oh, my, that's wonderful, yes it is, wonderful indeed!" declared Beatrice with a broad smile and dancing eyes as she looked from Bird to the children. As she looked about, Cord came around the corner of the building and stepped beside Bird.

"I wondered where you went. We need to pick out some more clothes for the youngsters."

Bird nodded, motioned the children to come with them, and the four walked back into the store to finish their gathering of goods, leaving Beatrice and Amy in the backyard, staring after them.

When they finished with the mercantile, they took the time to pack everything on the mule and in the panniers behind their saddles before readying to leave. An aproned man came from the mercantile and hailed Cord, "Say, you there," and came near. "My wife said you asked about some outlaws, Red Leg Bushwhacker type, that right?"

"I asked, yes."

"Ummhmm, well, I might be able to tell you somethin'," he began as he looked at the four that made up a bit of an unusual family group. The clerk frowned, then looked at Cord, "Bout three weeks ago, there was a bunch o' them come through here, did a little too much drinkin' and were gettin' a little mouthy and rough with some o' the regulars, you know, gold miners an' such, they got into a fight an' killed one o' them men, then took his horses and gear an' lit outta here like their pants was on fire. Never seen the like."

"How many were there?"

"Oh, maybe five or six, don't rightly remember. Rough lookin' bunch they was too."

"Don't you have any law hereabouts? You know, to go after 'em?"

"Yeah, we had a sheriff name o' Charley Pauls, but he resigned 'bout that time, an' when the next 'un took over, that was Ed Taylor, them fellas was gone! So, since the sheriff is just for this county, he din't go after 'em."

"And where'd they go?"

"Wal, they took off upriver, but don' know how far. Coulda kept goin' upriver, or turned north to go to South Park, hard tellin'."

"Can you tell me anything about 'em? You know, looks, horses, whatever."

"Only one I remember was one they called Red. He seemed to be the boss o' the bunch, big man, red hair, burly lookin'," the clerk shrugged.

"Well, I thank you for that. Gives me somethin' to go on anyway."

"Say, what'chu gonna do 'bout them kids?"

"Whaddaya mean?"

"Wal, Beatrice was sayin' you picked 'em up along the way, said their folks was killed an' you and your woman there was just helpin' 'em out."

"Yeah, and..." asked Cord, frowning.

The man took a deep breath, glanced around but no one seemed to be paying them much attention, and he stepped closer, "If you want, we might know of a couple families that would be glad to take 'em in, you know, like Beatrice there, she an' her man, Geoffrey, they're good people and they lost a boy here while back, got consumption and passed. They can't have no more children and I think they'd like more. Good folks, got a nice place out south of town, nice farmland, house, all that."

"We'll think about it. We'll be nearby for a day or

two and if we decide we want to go any further with that, we'll stop back in and talk."

The clerk smiled, stepped back, and nodded as he watched the four ride down the street and turn toward the river and the trees.

25

FAMILY

"Hello, the camp!" came a call from a man that had ridden to the tree line and stopped. He was alone and had one hand full of reins and the other held high and palm forward.

Cord answered, "C'mon in if you're friendly!"

The bay horse that looked more like a plow horse than breeding stock, stepped lively as the man dug heels in his ribs and moved into the little clearing where Cord and Bird had made their camp. Cord stood beside Bird who was sitting by the fire, cooking some bacon in the frying pan as the coffee pot danced on the rocks.

"Step down, have some coffee if you're of a mind."

"Pleased, thank you. I saw your smoke, figgered it was you folks. My wife told me about you and the young'uns." He looked at the two youngsters that sat on a log to the side of the fire. He looked back at

Cord, "I'm Baker Hatfield, you met muh wife yestiddy, our little one, Amy was playin' with your two young'uns, out back o' the mercantile."

"The clerk at the mercantile was tellin' me about your family," stated Cord, reaching for the coffee pot to pour both of them some coffee. "So, I s'pose you have a reason for coming out here this time of mornin'?"

"Yeah, muh missus sent me. After she talked to your woman about them kids, she couldn't stop talkin' 'bout it. We lost our son a little more'n a year back, consumption. He was older'n Amy, and muh missus ain't been the same since. Doc said she couldn't have no more kids and we had our hearts set on a big family." He paused, sipped some coffee, and added, "We got us a nice place, good land, had good crops so far, been there a couple years now. Built us a good house an' such. Had a big place 'fore the war, got burnt out and came west to start over." He looked up at Cord, glanced to Bird, and said, "So, if'n you was thinkin'..."

But Cord's uplifted hand stopped him as they looked to the wide-eyed twins who were listening and watching.

"Mr. Hatfield, it's not that we want to just leave the twins anywhere and with anyone. We've come to know them these past few days and they're very special young'uns. We've grown real fond of 'em and such, but we want what's best for them. That's the only reason we're talkin' now."

"Well, if'n you'd like, you all could come out to the home place, get a better idea what kind of home we're makin' and we can all talk about it, you know, all of us and the youngsters too, then decide. Think that'd be alright?"

Cord looked at Bird who gave a slight nod, then to the children to see their wide eyes showing a little fear, but they looked at one another, hugged each other close and Trey nodded and forced a smile. Cord looked to Baker Hatfield, and said, "All right, we'll come by, have a look and maybe talk, then decide." He paused and looked at Hatfield again, "But just because we're coming to look, does not obligate us in any way, understand? We want the twins to have the final say."

"Of course, of course," answered a grinning Hatfield as he jumped to his feet, "An' I'm sure the missus will want you to come for noon meal, if'n you would like."

Cord nodded, smiled, "We'll do that."

Cord and Bird rode in silence, the sun lowering in the west before them, the clear blue sky arching overhead, and the slight incline to the road most often used by the Barlow and Sanderson Stagecoach stretched before them. Their hearts were stirred by many different emotions - sadness, for the twins staying behind, happiness, for the bright future that lay before them, loneliness, due to their absence from the little entourage that had become a lot like family. Cord was thinking about what the Hatfields said about the new school being built in town and how excited all the families were about the new teacher, just arrived from St. Louis. It would be good for the children to have a better than average education, especially in these changing times.

Bird was thinking about how the children all bonded together, the twins and Amy, as if they had been family forever. It would be good for them to have a stable home, parents, and a sister. Trey was already proud of being a big brother and the girls agreed to gang up on their brother if needed, both giggling at the prospect.

"I was just remembering what my mother used to say, 'Sometimes it hurts to do what's right.'" Cord glanced to Bird and added, "But it was best for them."

Bird lifted her head, looked to Cord, and answered, "Yes, but it hurts."

Shortly after they crested the long hill to the west of Cañon City, a fork in the road held a sign pointing north that read Freshwater - 25 mi. and below that South Park - 45 mi. and below that board were two more, the first read Copper Gulch SS - 2 mi. the second read Texas Creek SS 14 mi. Bird frowned, "What does the SS mean?"

"Stage station. There's no towns there, just the station. That's what Hatfield was tellin' me right 'fore we left. He said there'd be a place to make camp down to the bottom, where a creek comes in from the north. We'll camp there tonight."

It was a little earlier than their usual camping time, but it afforded Cord time to try for some trout at the confluence of the creek and the Arkansas River. The creek was not very big, but the cooler water from the mountains was apparently a draw for the fish as Cord wasted little time in landing four nice sized rainbow trout. He quickly cleaned them and returned to their camp where the scrub oak sided some cottonwoods and Bird quickly had them in the pan for their supper.

As they sat back to enjoy the meal, Bird looked at Cord, "These men that you hunt, why?"

Cord paused a moment, finished the mouthful of trout, sipped some coffee, and began to explain, "That bunch did a lot of killing and burning during the war because they were supposedly fighting for freedom for the slaves, and maybe some of 'em were, but most were just outlaws out to rob and kill helpless people. The war was already over when they hit our place. I was off in the woods and by the time I got back, they had already killed my family, started the buildings burning, and were packing off all they could carry."

"That was many years ago?"

"Yes, almost three years ago."

"And you still want to find them?"

"Every day of my life and every thing I've done has been with the sole purpose of finding them and making them pay for what they did to my family and others," growled Cord, the muscles in his neck tensing and his eyes squinting as he clenched his teeth at the memories.

"But what about what you said to the preacher back at the fort, you know, about making things right between you and God, maybe forgiving others?"

Cord dropped his head, his chin to his chest as he slowly shook his head, then looked up at Bird with an embarrassed expression, "I know, but it's hard to do that after what they did. I know I should, and I keep talking to God about it, and I'm trying. I guess I really don't know what I'll do until I meet up with them."

"Does that mean you will still look for them?" asked Bird, her eyes pleading.

Cord took a deep breath, glancing away, "What they did is wrong, morally and legally, and when people do wrong they should face the consequences. Even if I find them and find it within me to forgive them, that does not make the wrong go away. They should pay for that." He shook his head as he thought about, and added, "When evil men do wrong, the only thing that will stop them is for good men to stand against them. That's true with your people and mine."

"Yes, but what about your life? Will you spend your life hunting them down? Don't you want to have a home and family, you know, like the Hatfield's?"

Cord looked at Bird, noticed she had a bit of a coy smile as she asked him that question, and he realized that she was thinking about the two of them making a family. He had to admit he had the same thoughts a time or two, but could they really do that? Could they have a life together, have a family, and more? He looked at the fire, the flames licking at the sticks and the hot coals glowing, then looked back at Bird, "Yes, I would like that, but..." he shrugged, set aside his plate and cup, stood and with a glance over his shoulder, said, "I'm gonna check on the horses."

26

CANYON

THE CANYON BEFORE THEM WAS DARK WITH THE SHADOWS of early morn. With the slow rising sun at their back, even the shadows of the horses stretched out before them. The hills on either side, freckled with piñon, cedar, and fir, also carried thickets of buck brush and cacti. The stagecoach road followed the river upstream, hugging the shoulders of the hills as they dropped into the riverbed, sometimes allowed just enough of a shoulder for the road, and that just wide enough for the stage and teams. But Cord and Bird were on the trail before any stagecoaches left Cañon City. They rode in silence, looking with awe at the amazing steep shouldered hills, some with escarpments of stone that seemed to rise from nowhere, while others were solid stone with shear cliffs standing on end with stubborn piñons clinging with tenuous roots in narrow crevices, but offering shelter to the occasional bighorn sheep, the only animal that could gambol among the rocks.

Cord suddenly reined up, held his hand to the side to stop Bird, then nodded ahead. Where the road made a bend around a low steep shoulder, a bunch of bighorn sheep were coming from on high for early morning water at river's edge. Cord had never seen a bighorn before and he was a little mesmerized as he watched two big rams, massive, curled horns looking like crowns, standing shoulder to shoulder, protecting the small bunch of ten, mostly ewes and new lambs with a few young rams, coming from the water and stretching out to climb the steep rocky slope and bounding from one rocky cleft to another, their hooves seemingly with glue as they mounted the shear obstacles as if they were common stairsteps. Cord and Bird remained immobile, the horses with lifted heads and pricked ears, all watching the unusual spectacle. When they were gone, Cord grinned, looked at Bird, "I ain't never seen the like! Those were magnificent creatures, bighorn sheep, weren't they?"

"Yes. They have good meat, their hides make soft leather, and the big horns are used by the people for many things," explained Bird, as they gigged the horses on.

They had come about seven or eight miles since their last camp and Cord heard the rattle of trace chains, the rumble of wheels, and the thunder of hooves behind them that told of a coming stagecoach. He nodded to the river's edge and told Bird, "Let's go down to the water, let the horses have a drink while the stage passes."

The Barlow and Sanderson Stage and Mail Line coach rumbled past just as Cord and Bird stepped down. The shotgunner waved as they passed, as did a couple passengers that were riding up top. Cord chuckled, looked at Bird, "Looks like they got a full load. Don't normally see folks up top like that, so it musta been full inside too." After the dust settled, Cord and Bird mounted up and resumed their journey west.

It was no more than four or five miles further on that Cord reined up when he heard a gunshot, then two more. He looked at Bird, "That was close." He looked about, saw a shoulder that stretched out from the steeper hillside, and pushed the road closer to the river, forcing it around the point. "Musta been around that bend." He pointed with his chin. He bent back to grab his binoculars from the saddlebags, slid to the ground and tossed Bird the reins of Kwitcher and the mule, and with rifle in hand, took the hillside in long strides. He hunkered down near the crest, bellied over the edge, and lifted the binoculars. The stage was stopped just below him, and four, no five, men were sitting their saddles in front of and beside the stage, all had pistols drawn, but one had a rifle laying across his pommel as he talked to the driver and the passengers, who had come from the stage and stood beside the stage, hands raised. Cord saw the mounted riders had neckerchiefs over their faces, and one man astride a big black, was waving his pistol as he apparently was shouting orders. The passengers began digging in pockets and reticules, retrieving any money and valuables, while the driver and messenger struggled with a locked strongbox from the forward boot of the stage.

Cord lowered the binoculars just as a rustling behind him caught his attention and he turned to see Bird, scampering up beside him, rifle in hand. He spoke softly to her, "Highwaymen, robbing the stage and passengers. We need to stop them. You scoot over behind that rock, and if I shoot, you shoot, but first I'll try to stop them."

He watched as Bird took cover behind the big boulder, then he lifted his rifle, took careful aim at the rifle held in the hand of the one man, and squeezed off his shot. They were about thirty yards from the outlaws, maybe thirty feet above them, and when the Henry bucked and roared, the thunder racketed across the narrow gorge, sounding more like a barrage of several rifles. The bullet flew true and splintered the forestock of the outlaw's rifle and Cord hollered, "Drop 'em 'fore we cut loose on all of you! We've got you covered!"

But there's always at least one in a bunch that thinks he's faster, better, and even invulnerable. The man on the black that had been ordering the others turned and opened fire on the hillside. But Cord and Bird were well covered, and as they both returned fire, emptying two saddles, and wounding two others that clung to their saddles as they slumped over the pommels. The horses had spooked, and all the riders fought to bring them under control, giving the shotgun messenger time to grab his coach gun and cut down on the leader, blasting him out of the saddle. One of the wounded men had dug heels into his horse and disappeared into a narrow draw that cut between the hills.

When the shooting started, the passengers hit the ground, a couple of women crawled under the coach while the others hunkered together behind the coach. When no more gunfire came from below, Cord and Bird quickly returned to their horses where Bird had tethered them to a twisted cedar beside the road and rode around the bend to come alongside the stagecoach. The driver had wrapped the lines around the brake handle and was helping the passengers from their cover and into the coach and when he saw Cord and Bird, he grinned and walked to them, "Boy howdy, you two sure saved the day! I thought those outlaws were gonna kill us all! And when you opened up, it sounded like an angel from Heaven, yessir!"

Cord chuckled, "I've been called a lot of things, but never an angel."

The driver turned and pointed to the draw beyond the stage, "The one that got away, disappeared into that draw, if'n you wanna go after him."

"Why would I wanna do that?" asked Cord, leaning on his pommel.

"Uh, ain'tchu a lawman?"

"No, not hardly."

"That'd be me," came a voice from behind Cord.

Cord twisted around in his saddle to see two men riding up to the stage. One man looked at the driver and asked, "So, what happened here, Mort?"

"Wal, howdy, Sheriff," answered the driver, "Just what it looks like. These men,"—he motioned to the three bodies, and one man sitting on the ground, leaning against the front wheel of the coach, holding his bleeding shoulder and wincing—"were tryin' to rob the stage, and this man"—pointing to Cord and Bird—"stopped 'em."

The sheriff looked at Cord and Bird, stepped down and walked among the dead and wounded, came back beside Cord, looked up at him and said, "Well?"

"Well what?" answered Cord, confusion showing on his face.

"You were askin' in town about some men that were Bushwhackers or Red Legs, and Wicker at the mercantile told you about 'em."

"That's right, so?"

The sheriff turned, pointed to the dead man that had been dropped by the shotgunner, "That's one of 'em."

Cord looked quickly toward the downed man, swung down, and walked close. He stood over the bloody body that had taken the full shotgun blast, dead center, from the messenger. But his face was untouched as Cord pulled the neckerchief away. He looked at the man, shaking his head, remembering. This was one of the few he could recognize, he had the way of a dandy about him, always dressed in black, fancy rigs, leather vest, hat, and gloves, but now most was red. Cord pulled a slip of paper from his pocket and a stub of a pencil, opened the paper, and crossed out the name *Dave Poole*. He tucked away the paper and pencil, walked back to his horse and swung aboard. With a nod to Bird, they rode away from the stage, continuing west on the stage road.

Mort, the driver, looked at Sheriff Taylor, "Talkative sort, ain't he?"

The sheriff just shook his head, then asked, "Did any of the outlaws get away?"

"One did, but I don't think he'll go far. Looked like he was hit purty bad." The driver stepped away from the coach, pointed to the draw beyond and said, "He went up that draw, last I saw."

"They didn't get the strongbox?"

"Nope, shore din't! Thanks to that feller and his squaw."

27

MOUNTAINS

They rode past the Texas Creek Stage station with a wave and a nod, found a place for their nooning at the edge of the river a few miles further along. But the day was warm, blue sky, and bright sunshine and the trail beckoned. They pushed on enjoying the ride and the always changing scenery, with piñon freckled hills showing jutting rock-laden shoulders, scampering mule deer, occasional coyotes, and mischievous long-eared rabbits. Occasionally, because of sheer cliffs that rose abruptly from the river and offered nothing in the way of a shoulder, the trail left the river to move north up a draw, cross over a saddle and drop back to the river canyon by another gravel bottomed draw.

The stage road took the eyebrow trail around a big steep bluff, and the canyon suddenly opened up into a long grass bottomed valley and standing like a garrison of uniformed soldiers rose the Sangre de

Cristo mountain range that marched into the north-west distance. The blue skirts of deep timber lay like a warm blanket while granite tipped peaks scratched the blue of the azure sky, yet in the deep crevices and gulches, white snow showed like the decorative cords and braids that hung from the broad shoulders of the uniformed garrison.

Cord and Bird reined up to take in the amazing scene with the grey tipped peaks with black timber rising so high above them, and the deep green forests of the foothills that bordered the serene beauty of the grasslands between the river and the mountains. As they sat, taking it all in, a herd of elk tiptoed from the trees, moved into the deep grass, and began to graze. They were the royalty of the land, standing head and shoulders above the mule deer, stately racks showing velvet as they grew, and the dusty blonde rumps that twisted among the brush usually in pursuit of orange colored calves.

They reveled in the majesty and beauty as Cord said, "This is the high country I dreamed about. That range of mountains, the Sangre de Cristo, I've heard about them and pictured them, but never like this. It's said the name, Sangre de Cristo, means the Blood of Christ and they were named by black robe missionaries that were here many years ago. I don't know where they got that name, but..." he shrugged, grinning as he glanced to Bird.

Bird said, "In the evening, when the sun sets, it often casts a glow on the snow covered peaks that looks red. That is why the priests said it was the Blood of Christ. I never understood that before, but now, after what we did back at the fort with the preacher, I understand why it is so important." She looked at Cord, "This *is* high country, but some of my people live beyond those mountains, and others more to the north where there is another mountain range that is even bigger than these mountains."

"Bigger than these? I've got to see them." He gigged Kwitcher forward as they broke from the mouth of the canyon into the long, beautiful valley that stretched beyond the limits of their eyesight. Within a couple miles, they came to the Pleasant Valley Stage Station and stopped to visit with the keeper and his helper. It was getting late in the day and when the men pointed out a thicket of cotton-woods at a bend in the river, Cord and Bird moved on, choosing the thicket for the camp for the night.

They were up and moving before the sun bent its rays over the mountains to warm their backs. It was another clear day and as the darkness retreated from the rising sun, the lone star in the darkness that hung over the western horizon twinkled its good day to the travelers. The stage road showed recent travel of the day before, and the cool of the morning beck-oned the early risers to come to the river for their morning drink. The valley stretched out to the north and south of the river, and lay like a carpet of green to the west, offering an easy course for the young river, much smaller now than when they first sided the Arkansas earlier in the journey. The mountains of the Sangre de Cristo range continued their march to the northwest, a long line of granite tipped peaks that stood proudly along the western edge of the valley. There had been a sign beside the road near the Pleasant Valley Stage Station that said the next station, Cleora, was twenty-one miles to the west-northwest.

The keeper at the Pleasant Valley station said, "Yeah, the next station is a bit further'n most, twenty-one mile, but it ain't bad travelin'. Follers the river all the way, there's a bit of a canyon, but it opens up into a big, wide valley that makes this'n look like a skimpy little meadow. An' after that it turns north and goes all the way to Oro City, don' rightly know why, cuz that gold field done played out, but who'm I ta' judge?"

They had ridden about seven or eight miles, the sun now shone on their right shoulders and backs, as the rode bent around a shoulder of a butte and the valley opened wide before them. With the river having cut its way through the valley floor and was now a good twenty feet below the shoulder of the road, the valley floor stretched a couple miles to the west before rising up the bluff of the wide flat plateau, but Cord reined up, holding his hand to the side to stop Bird. She looked where he stared and beyond the valley floor riding across the flat of the plateau, was a band of natives numbering about twenty.

Cord leaned back to slip his binoculars from the saddlebags and lifted them for a better look. "Doesn't look like they're wearin' paint, but they aren't hunting in a bunch like that."

"Maybe it's not game they're hunting," offered Bird, shading her eyes to look into the distance. She extended her hand for the binoculars and Cord passed them to her. She lifted them for a better look, "Those are Comanche, that is a raiding party. They are either going to strike a settler, or some of my people."

"We won't know what they're headin' for until we see it. The station keeper back yonder said there ain't much 'tween here and Cleora and there ain't much at Cleora." He paused, watching Bird's reaction to the warriors. She lowered the glasses and returned them to Cord. "I don't know how this valley lays and if we're even headin' the same place, but we can try to get there 'fore they do, maybe give a warning to whoever they're after."

He replaced the binoculars and with a glance to Bird, kicked Kwitcher up to a trot. He was trying to keep under cover wherever possible, although he did not believe they were in any danger from the Comanche who were on the southwest side of the river and a good two miles away, but it was always best to not expose yourself when there was any possibility of danger. Kwitcher and the white mare of Bird's enjoyed stretching out and when Cord gave Kwitcher his head, he picked up the pace and with his face in the wind, his mane and tail flying, he led the way as the trio of animals thundered across the flats.

Cord soon pulled the big stallion back to a trot and then to a walk, letting the animals have a breather as they settled down to a good walk, still stretching their legs and feeling good. He kept up that changing pace for a good twelve or fourteen miles then turned from the road to the river bottom where another mountain stream fed into the bigger river. The horses and mule dipped their noses into the water, as Cord and Bird went to one knee and scooped up handfuls of water for themselves. Cord stood, looked around, back down the trail and across the river where the hills had pushed in toward the river, forcing any travelers on that side to take to the narrow riverbank or cross the river to the northeast side where Cord and Bird were, to continue west. There was an obvious trail that rode above the water, keeping to the shoulder of the mountains and rocky escarpments, turning into an eyebrow trail in places, but still passable. Cord looked at Bird, "We're ahead of 'em, if they're still coming this way, so I think we need to give the animals a breather, maybe have a little somethin' for ourselves, before goin' any further."

———

DUSK WAS JUST DROPPING its curtain when they came from the canyon into the valley that lay before the bigger mountain range that Bird remembered from her childhood. Before them stretched a mountain range that stood proudly with its granite tipped peaks and marched to the north beyond their line of sight. But just a short distance before them stood the stage station of Cleora. Bigger than most with a two-story wood plank building that held the station, a trading post, a café, and a hotel. The south side had a full-length porch, while the back of the building held the livery and corrals for the stage teams. Cord looked at Bird, back at the station, grinned and said, "Maybe we'll just eat in the café and if'n you want, we can stay in the hotel." He nodded to the west, "Those clouds are showin' a little bit of lightnin' and it might just get wet tonight, so a hotel room might be just what we need." Bird nodded and as Cord nudged Kwitcher toward the building, he noticed a big sign across the front that said Bale's Station.

When they reined up, they were greeted by a crusty old-timer with a drooping moustache that covered his upper lip and hung below his chin. "Howdy folks! Gonna git outta the weather, are ye?"

"Thought about it. But we also wanted to..." but he was interrupted by the arrival of a stage from the north wheeling in and coming to a stop. The driver hollered, "Hey, we got us a wounded man here! Give us some help!" He tied off the lead lines to the brake handle, climbed down, and jerked open the door.

Cord went to help, and the messenger, driver, and Cord lifted a man from inside that wore a bloody homespun shirt and the stub of an arrow shaft protruding from his shoulder. Cord asked, "Comanche?"

The driver responded, "No! Cheyenne, I think. But we lost another'n. We had stopped at the water when they hit us. Couldn't get that'n in, but he was done fer' anyway. Don' know why they din't foller us, we got away, but we made some dust in the doin' of it!"

They carried the man into the station, and Cord returned to where Bird awaited. They led the horses to the livery, rented some stalls and stripped the gear, stacking it in the corner of the stall with the mule. Cord told Blue to stay with the horses and he dug him a bed in the hay, looked at Cord with a pitiful look and watched as they left. They carried their bedrolls and weapons with them when they returned to the hotel, stepped inside and up to the counter. Cord said, "We need two rooms, adjoining if you got 'em."

"Two rooms? That mean you want one fer her?"

"One for her, one for me."

"But she's a injun!" declared the man, disgust showing on his face.

"She's a woman, and my friend," declared Cord, cocking one eyebrow up as he gave a defiant look to the mousy clerk.

The man cowered, stepped back and pushed the

register toward Cord. "That'll be two dollars!" he declared, glancing from Cord to Bird.

"And I'll want some fresh water in both rooms, please."

Cord lay the coin on the counter, accepted the keys, and led Bird up the stairs to the rooms. He opened the room for Bird, led her in and looked it over, letting her sit on the bed as he did. He looked at her, "Soon as you're ready, come downstairs and we'll go to the café to eat."

Bird smiled, nodded, and began unrolling her bedroll.

28

INFORMATION

WHEN CORD CAME DOWN TO THE CAFÉ TO AWAIT BIRD, HE was seated at a window table and looking outside when he noticed the north bound stage that came from Cañon City, was sitting beside the one that came from the north carrying the wounded man. As he waited, he looked around the café, if it could be called that, it was more the eating room for the stage passengers during a layover/change of teams, and there were several of the passengers seated at the other tables, most already busy with their food.

The driver and messenger from the northbound stage walked in, saw Cord and both came over to his table, "Howdy! Say, it shore is good to see you. You got away without us even gittin' a chance to say thanks fer what you done down the line earlier." The driver extended his hand and said, "Let me shake yore hand, friend. Ain't often I git to say thankee to someone fer savin' muh life!"

Cord accepted the man's hand and nodded, glancing to the messenger and around the room, looking for Bird. He caught a glimpse of movement at the door between the hotel and the café, frowned, and slowly stood to look at Bird coming into the room. She had doffed her buckskins and now wore a long, gathered floor length dark-blue skirt, a white Victorian puffed sleeve blouse, and a broad smile beneath her loose hair that was tucked behind her ears and hung over her shoulders. She had made a trade with the sutler at Fort Lyon and had tucked away the package in her bedroll without showing Cord. She was beautiful and a bit timid as she spotted Cord and started in his direction. When the two men saw Cord looking that way, they turned to look as well, and they too showed broad smiles as Bird came to the table. Cord motioned her to the chair he held for her, and the men watched as she was seated. Cord looked at the two, motioned to the other two seats and they readily accepted the offer.

When all were seated, the two men looked at Bird and the driver spoke, "Ma'am, we was just thankin' your friend here for jumpin' in for us this mornin' when them outlaws hit, and we want to thank you too. You did just as much as he did, and if'n you two hadn't been there, we might be still layin' in the road back there."

Bird just smiled, nodded, and looked to Cord, who lightly touched her hand to reassure her. He looked to the men, "We were here when the south bound came in with that wounded passenger. How's he doin'?"

"He din't make it. They said it was a band o' Cheyenne. That could spell trouble for us tomorrow on the run up to California Gulch n' Oro City."

"There's also a band of 'bout twenty or so Comanche headin' this way. They were kinda shadowin' your coach on the way here," stated Cord, leaning back for the waitress to place the coffee cups around the table and to fill the cups with steaming coffee.

The driver frowned, looked at Cord, "You sure 'bout that?"

"Ummhmm, we saw 'em 'fore we saw you. They were on the south side of the river, went up into the hills and were stayin' a good distance south. But they were comin' upstream and had scouts out watchin' the stage."

The driver looked at his messenger and back to Cord, "You think they'd hit the station here?"

"Dunno. Lost sight of 'em after the river ducked into the canyon this last stretch."

Bird spoke, "With the Cheyenne coming from the northeast, and the Comanche from the southeast, perhaps they will meet. Or they could join with the Caputa or Mouache Ute, maybe have a buffalo hunt, or a war parley."

The driver shook his head, ran his fingers through his hair and said, "I was just gettin' used to havin' all this hair!"

The others chuckled, leaned back for the delivery of their plates of food and Cord asked, "How soon you headin' out?"

"Right'chere in a little while. Soon's they git the team all lined out an' the passengers on board," explained the messenger.

"Are you gonna be goin' north on the stage road?" asked the driver, glancing to Cord.

Cord grinned, "My name is Cordell Beckett, Cord for short, and this is Yellow Singing Bird, or Bird. And no, probably not. We are headin' to the land of the Caputa Ute, looking for Bird's family. She was stolen from the Ute when she was just a youngster, and we'll be trying to find them."

The driver grinned, "And I'm Alex MacPherson and this,"—nodding to the messenger—"is Charlie Lehman." He paused and continued, "So you two," began the driver, motioning to Cord and Bird, "aren't, you know, married?"

Cord chuckled, grinned, "No, we're just friends. I agreed to bring her with me when we met up back on the trail right after we came along the Arkansas River."

"Then good luck to you both. And you watch your topknot, what with all them restless natives, you know, the Cheyenne, the Comanche, and even some o' them Ute out and about, gotta be careful!" The two men rose, reached down to take the last sip of coffee, then with a nod and a wave, left the café.

Cord looked to Bird, "You ready to leave?"

Cord led the way as they stepped out onto the long veranda of the hotel/mercantile/stage stop known as *Bale's Station*. He stood enjoying the warmth of the morning sun until a man stepped near, "Say, ain'tchu the one whut helped out ol' MacPherson down nigh Copper Gulch?"

Cord turned to look at the man, nodded, "You could say that."

"I'm Otis Elmer, I drive the southbound, an' they was sayin' you had been a mite curious 'bout one o' dem outlaws, the one whut was fancied up and known to be one o' dem Red Legs. Said you was lookin' fer others like him, that right?"

"That's right," answered Cord, frowning.

"Wal, thought you might wanna know, I run into some hyar a while back. An' I heard some others talkin' 'bout 'em. Seems they was known to be up the North Fork of the Little Arkansas, place some ol' sourdoughs was callin' Shavano, after the name o' that mountain with the angel on it. Then I heard others say they was some of 'em up Chalk Creek. There's some new diggin's up thataway an' they was known to be stayin' in a ol' cabin left empty by another sourdough."

"Shavano?"

"Yeah, lookee yonder," said Otis, stepping to the edge of the veranda and pointing to the mountains on the west edge of the wide valley that stretched out before them. "Them mountains yonder, that big'n with the high peak and smaller peaks on either side," he paused and looked to Cord, waiting for an acknowledgment of seeing the mountain. After he nodded, Otis continued, "See there in that draw 'tween the first peak and the tallest one? Notice the way the snow lays in those wrinkles, see that? Looks just like an angel with wide spread wings, don' it?"

Cord frowned, "Yeah, I reckon it does. That's somethin'."

The driver chuckled, "They call that the Angel of Shavano, cuz that's the name o' the mountain. I ain't got the time now, but sometime ya' oughta get somebody local to tell you the legend of that angel. Anyhoo, to the left, or south of that mountain, the North Fork of the Little Arkansas comes from up there. Some ol' sourdoughs thot they'd find gold up thataway and built 'em a cabin or two, then left it for other diggin's. I heard them Redlegs was known to be up there. But if'n you're thinkin' of goin' up there after 'em, I would not advise it. That's mighty rough, steep, country an' you ain't gonna sneak up on anybody up there."

"Well, thanks anyway," offered Cord, shaking hands with the driver and stepping off the porch with Bird to go to the livery for the animals.

The sun was just climbing over the eastern hills when they rode from Cleora and *Bale's Station*. The stage road hugged the flanks of the foothills that were sprinkled with juniper and piñon, with the lower skirts showing an abundance of sage and greasewood. But as the shoulders of the foothills pushed toward the river, the road bent to make a crossing just upstream of the confluence with the stream most locals were calling Little River, the South Arkansas. The crossing was wide, shallow, and gravel bottomed, made so by the stage company and the eons of time with the river washing across the flats. A smattering of cottonwoods marked the east bank, and willows and cottonwoods stood proudly on the west bank. Once across, they climbed the bank and came out on the wide flat that stretched to the west and north.

Off their left shoulder, the beginning of the south bound Sangre de Cristos, showed the beginning of the mountain range that stretched south into the New Mexico territory and showed as a spine that divided the east and west plains of the Colorado Territory. But where the Sangre de Cristo ended, the Sawatch Range began its long march north with mountains that stood even taller than those of the Sangres. Cord looked at the deep cut valley that lay to the south of the mountain the driver Otis called Shavano, and a wide flat-top mesa lay below a solitary mountain to the south of Shavano, but beyond the foothills at the end of the Sangres.

Bird stood in her stirrups, pointing to the lowlands between the mountain ranges, "I remember that! Our people used to cross there and sometimes stop at the hot springs. When we had a buffalo hunt to the south, we would come back to those mountains, make camp in the flats below the black timber"—she moved her hand as she spoke, pointing out the different ranges and flatlands— "and I remember one time when we came this way" —she twisted in her saddle and pointed to the north —"and just past that pointed hill, the one without many trees and stands pointing like an anthill, and there's a trail there that takes you through these mountains and beyond to a place with many hot springs. We would spend winter there." She dropped back into her saddle, smiling at the memories, glanced to Cord and saw he too was smiling with her memories.

"You think your people might be somewhere over there," nodding to the Sawatch Range.

"Perhaps, or we might find sign."

Cord grinned, nudged Kwitcher to the chosen route and with a taut line on the mule, Blue beside them, they started west.

29

PONCHA SPRINGS

THEY FOLLOWED THE LITTLE RIVER, STAYING TO THE NORTH bank and within the tree line whenever possible. Cord's mind was busy with all the reports he had learned regarding the native activity. The Cheyenne that had hit the stage north of Cleora, the Comanche they had spotted on the flanks of the Sangre de Cristo mountains, the possibility of the encampment of the Caputa Ute, and the proximity of the cabins used by the Red Legs. With this broad valley, it was possible for all the different peoples to never encounter any others, but... he shrugged as he thought about it. A quick glance to Bird showed her excitement about being in the land of her people and the possibility of finding them was very real. Cord grinned, and knew for her sake, he hoped they did find her people and anything else would just have to find its own time and place.

He looked through the thin cottonwoods, across the little river, and thought he saw movement. He held out his hand to Bird and bent low on his horse's neck to peer through the foliage. He turned and whispered to Bird, "Comanche, there," pointing across the river, and slid to the ground, rifle in hand. Bird did the same and stood beside Cord, looking where he pointed and saw what they guessed to be the same band they had spotted near Copper Gulch, at the mouth of the canyon of the Arkansas.

The band was moving silently, weapons in hand, cautious as they moved, but not on a hunt. They split the trees and crossed the river upstream of where Cord and Bird stood, watching. Cord counted twenty-three warriors, painted for battle. Cord looked at their back trail, saw they had come from a draw that split the foothills and probably came over the foothills that lay in the shadows of the Sangres from the south. They moved across the grassy flats, bound to the north toward a low-rising flat mesa that extended for several miles from the west to the east. They waited until the band had crossed the flats and mounted the mesa and disappeared.

Cord looked at Bird, shook his head, "Now that looks like trouble!"

Bird nodded, stepped back aboard her mare as Cord straddled Kwitcher and they continued westward. The land on either side of the little river showed an abundance of green, tall grasses, waving in the morning breeze. They passed a couple log homes, probably settlers that were making their land into a farm with plowed ground all around and rows of seedlings pushing their heads through the black soil. On the flats north of the river, Cord saw a clapboard house, two stories, sitting among a cluster of trees, with other outbuildings about. He was surprised to see the structures, and what appeared to be a well-established ranch. A little farther on, the trees were thicker and the grassland less. A cluster of cabins showed what might be the beginnings of a town and one cabin, a little larger than the others and with a free-standing shelter beside it, had a sign across the doorway, Trading Post, John Burnett, Indian Agent. Cord pointed it out, nudged Kwitcher to the hitchrail, and both stepped down.

A man stepped into the doorway, "Mornin'!" he declared, holding his pipe in his hand as the little wisp of smoke twisted upward. He was a clean-shaven man, dark wavy hair, linen shirt, homespun trousers held up with galluses, and a broad smile. He glanced to Bird, back to Cord, "So, what brings you by this way on such a fine day?"

"Oh, a little tradin', a little palaver," began Cord, leaning back against the hitchrail, and looking at the man. "You the Indian Agent?"

"That's right, John Burnett," offered the man, stepping forward and extending his hand to shake.

Cord responded in kind, "I'm Cordell Beckett,

and this is Yellow Singing Bird. We're looking for her people, the Caputa Ute, know anything about 'em?"

"I do, I'm the appointed agent for the Caputa and the Mouache Ute people. They come in often to trade, to get their annuities, and more. Last I heard, the Caputa under Ouray and his wife Chipeta were camped just over in the San Luis Valley, back that-away," pointing to the cut between the foothills to the south. "But we often have different ones come in to trade just about any time. And I also heard that War Chief Colorow and some of his Weenuchiu, come from o'er the Roaring Fork an' Gunnison country, are somewhere hereabouts also. Don't reckon he an' his boys are just huntin'. They been known to kick up a ruckus wherever they be."

Cord glanced to Bird, saw her happy face at the news of the Caputa, then looked back to Burnett, "I also heard about some outlaw types, Bushwhackers, Red Legs, that might be holed up farther into the mountains, near the headwaters of the north fork of the South Arkansas. Hear anything like that?"

"Why are you lookin' for trouble of that kind?"

"Got a debt to settle," growled Cord, leaving no doubt of his intentions as he looked at Burnett.

"Yeah, I heard that, but don't believe it. I know that country and there ain't any reason why those types would be up there. Sides, if they were, I'da heard about 'em from the Utes, they keep track of all the newcomers. Matter o' fact, I heard you was comin' two days ago," he chuckled, enjoying the surprised look on Cord's face. "Now, I did hear 'bout some o' them types bein' up Chalk Creek, which seems more likely, but even that I'd put the doubt to." He paused, relit his pipe and looked at Cord through the cloud of smoke, "Yuh see, prospectin' is hard work, and that type don't go in for hard work. Now, if'n I was them, I'd be headin' upriver to California Gulch, or Oro City, that valley up yonder has had some good strikes, likely to have more. And if they're lookin' to lift some pokes from unsuspectin' prospectors, that's where they'd find 'em."

Cord nodded, turned to look about, "Looks like you've got a growin' community hereabouts. Ranches, farms, and such, shows promise."

Burnett grinned, nodding, "It does. New people comin' in all the time. The Hendricks and the Rich's were the first families hereabouts, the Rich's already had a son born to 'em, James, born just last year. Down the valley yonder, the Hutchinson's have a nice ranch, and the McPherson's got 'em a farm goin'. McPherson's gonna put in a grocery store yonder, that's them makin' all the noise buildin'. And up the hill yonder, Henry Weber and Paul Irvine and me are puttin' in a hot springs bath, which will be mighty comfortin' after a hard day's work." He stuck his thumbs under his galluses, pulled them out as he puffed on his pipe, talking out of the side of his mouth and grinning proudly.

Cord grinned, looking about the trading post and

back to Burnett, "When was the last time you had trouble with the natives?"

Burnett stood up, reached for his pipe, and scowled at Cord, "What're you getting' at?"

"We saw a band of Comanche a couple days back, and again 'bout three, four miles down this valley this mornin'. Painted for war, they were, but they looked to be headin' north." Cord watched Burnett's reaction to the news of the Comanche, then continued, "And that ain't all. We spent the night at Bale's Station, and the stage from the north came in with a wounded man, said they had been hit by some Cheyenne."

Burnett dropped his eyes, shaking his head, "Not good, not good," he mumbled, until the sound of another rider came from below the other cabins. He looked up to see a familiar figure approach, and he raised a hand, "Mornin' Joe!" as the man stepped down with a somber expression painting his face. He nodded to Burnett, glanced to Cord and Bird, back to Burnett. "We might have trouble comin'," he began, "There was a band of what I think were Comanche that crossed my lower pasture a little bit ago. They was headed north across the valley, but I didn't stick around long to make sure. Thought I better let folks know, maybe we could get somethin' together, just in case."

"I know," replied Burnett, glancing from Joe to Cord and back.

Joe frowned, looked at Burnett, "You know?

How'd you know, they just crossed, an' I came straightaway."

"Joe, this is Cordell Beckett and Yellow Singing Bird. Cord, this is Joe Hutchinson, one of the early settlers hereabouts." Cord and Hutchinson shook hands and Burnett added, "They saw that band a couple days back on the stage road, and again when they crossed Little River and your pasture. They came to tell me about 'em."

Joe looked from Burnett to Cord and asked, "You know anything else about 'em we need to know?"

"Only that they were wearin' war paint," explained Cord. "We did our best to avoid 'em." He looked from Joe to Burnett and back, "We're,"— nodding to Bird—"lookin' for the Caputa Ute, her people."

Joe looked to Burnett, "So, what do you think? About the Comanche, I mean."

Burnett shook his head, "That's not all of it. According to Cord here, the stage from Oro City came into Bale's with a wounded man, they said had been hit by Cheyenne. And..." he paused, shaking his head, "I got word that War Chief Colorow of the Weenuchiu, has a band, don't know how big, campin' out on the Cochetopa."

"Comanche, Cheyenne, Ute Mountain Ute, ain't none of 'em friendly with the others and all comin' together somewhere near here!" grumbled Hutchinson, shaking his head. "We gotta do sumpin'. Hopefully they'll just kill each other, but if that fight comes thisaway, we need to be ready!"

"Ummhmm, what do you recommend?" asked Burnett, looking to the man that was considered by most to be the leader of the community, seeing as how he was one of the first settlers.

"Let's get the others together, you go that way, I'll go this, we'll all meet back here."

30

TRAVELERS

THE LEADER OF THE YAMPARIKA COMANCHE WAS THE WAR chief, *Ah-te-es-ta*, Little Horn. On their sweep through the southern foothills several of the *Waha-Toya*—Foothills in the Clouds people—had joined them, but Little Horn was the unquestioned leader. Little Horn looked to his sub chief, *Quirts-quip*, Chewing Elk, who had taken the name of his father after he was lost in battle, to hear the report from the scouts.

"The scouts tell of a band of Cheyenne Dog Soldiers that have hit a stage, but lost them. They have also attacked a ranch and stolen horses from the ranch and the stage company. They have four hands of warriors."

"How many horses have they taken?"

"Three hands, but they had others before they attacked the ranch."

"When we strike, you will lead two hands to circle around and come from behind. We will attack from the bluff as they come below us."

Elk grinned, "Will we return to our people through the valley of San Luis, and strike the camp of the Ute for more horses?"

"We will take all their horses and return to our people with a great herd," Little Horn said with a wide grin and a belly laugh.

"It is good," declared Elk, as he nodded to the edge of the bluff where just the tops of the cotton-woods showed the valley of the Arkansas where they expected to find the Cheyenne.

Little Horn had led such raids before and had always returned with many horses and other plunder that enriched his warriors. As his band came from the waters of the South Arkansas and crossed the grasslands of the valley, they had spotted the horse herds of the white settlers and were deter-mined to take them on their return. With the approach of the Cheyenne, they decided they would wait before striking the settlers of the flats, going against the Cheyenne would be their first strike. When they wiped out the Cheyenne, then they would strike other ranches, take the horses and plunder, and they would turn south, go through the San Luis Valley, go against the Ute, and take some buffalo before returning to their village beyond the Sangre de Cristos.

WHEN WHITE ANTELOPE was but a young man, barely into his teens, he protected his mother and little sister and helped them escape the massacre at Sand Creek, but White Antelope's father, with the same name, was killed defending his people. He was one of the few warriors that charged the soldiers and shot them before being repeatedly shot by the charging cavalry. Young White Antelope had seen his father fall from his hidden vantage in the deep gulch north of the encampment, but there was no mistaking his father, the valiant warrior he had always been known to be, brave in life and even braver in death. But his death had embittered young White Antelope, and he was determined to avenge the death of his father that had been brought about by the traitorous white soldiers. Now he rode beside Howling Wolf, a proven warrior and leader of the war parties made up of similar minded *Hesé'omeétaneo'o,* Cheyenne Dog Soldiers who would not lay down their weapons for the treaties that were never honored by the white men. They had come across South Park, striking the few cabins of the white men that dug for the gold metal and leaving their desecrated bodies behind. They crossed the foothills on the west and dropped into the valley of the Arkansas River that lay at the foot of the Sawatch Mountains. They had attacked the stage station and a fleeing stage, but the stage had fresh horses and theirs were tired from a long days ride and the stage escaped, but they burned the station and killed the white men, taking eight horses as the beginning of their plunder. After the stage station, they took a ranch, killed everyone, burned the buildings, and stole another dozen horses. They retreated to the river bottom, made camp for the night and with an early start, they would go south along the river, take any other ranchers or settlers, relieve them of their horses and any plunder, then cross over the south end of the valley, take the pass to the San Luis Valley and strike the Utes to take captive women and horses before returning to their village, but for now, they would go to camp in the trees along the river, it had been a long day and they and their horses were tired.

Howling Wolf awakened White Antelope, "Our scouts say we have been spotted by the scouts of some Comanche."

"How many?"

"They do not know. The Comanche were in the thick trees as they crossed from the south end of the valley."

"Were they seen?"

"They say no."

"Send them out again, see how many Comanche. If we can take them, we will, but if too many..." he shrugged as he came from his blankets.

———

COLOROW, often called the red Indian, even by some of his own, was the war leader of the Weenuchiu Ute people, rode at the front of the long procession of the people, warriors, families, women leading horses laden with packs and dragging travois. His people were on the move from the Roaring Fork valley and the land of the Gunnison, now bound for the north, and Mount Vernon where he had many friends among the settlers and townspeople. The band numbered in the hundreds and the horse herd had even more horses than there were people in the band. Colorow turned to look back at the cavalcade of Ute Mountain people, proud of his people. He looked beside him where Chief Nevava rode, leading his own people who had joined with Colorow and his Weenuchiu. His thoughts turned to the joining of the bands.

Chief Nevava rode into the light of the campfire, four warriors following, and greeted Colorow with the usual greeting of the Ute, "*Makwa,*" as he held his right hand high, palm forward.

"Makwa," responded Colorow, also holding his hand high, "*Niyapö.*"

Nevava nodded, swung his leg over the rump of his mount, nodding to his warriors and they also stepped down.

Nevava came to face Colorow, and asked, "*Mana'nanakwa   maavaa   pa'ag   süümaratüm nanapükaan?*"

"Yes, we travel to the north to our summer encampment. Do your people want to join us?" asked Colorow.

"Our scouts have told of Cheyenne Dog Soldiers that come from the north, and Comanche that come from the south. Perhaps they go against one another, but if we are joined, we will be too formidable for them to come against us," explained Nevava.

"It is good," responded Colorow, always one to seek peace, but also willing to fight if the prize was great and with many honors. Colorow saw his leaders, White Skunk and Big Turtle nodding their agreement, as did the leaders with Nevava.

Now as he looked at the convoy of Ute people, dust began to lift from the trail and the morning breeze from the high mountains off their left shoulder, moved the dust across the valley that lay between the Arkansas River and the South Arkansas, or Little River. The vast valley stretched its green carpet to the east where the Arkansas River carved its way to the narrow canyon where it would escape to the east. Where the Ute rode was atop the long alluvial plain that came from the Sawatch mountains and lay above the river valleys. Where the rivers meandered, cottonwoods, burr oak, and random aspen marked the way, but that way was below the shoulders of the wide mesa of the plain.

Colorow looked to Nevava, "Let us gather our warriors. Leave the young ones and the old ones with the people, we will prepare for the Comanche and the Cheyenne."

"It is good," declared Nevava as both leaders signaled their sub chiefs to rally the warriors together.

31

CONFLICT

THE VALLEY OF THE ARKANSAS RIVER AND THE SOUTH
Arkansas, or Little River, formed a triangle with the
upper point lying in the north, the southeastern
point at the confluence of the two rivers, and the
southwestern point toward the headwaters of Little
River to the west of Poncha Springs, a distance of
about ten miles and each side of the triangular valley
being about the same distance. The alluvial fan that
formed the flat-topped mesa came from the flanks of
the Sawatch foothills that bordered the line from the
southwest corner to the northernmost point. The tip
of that fan pushed toward the river but stopped
short although well within sight of the stage road
that traveled from Cleora in the southeastern point,
along the foothills that rode the east bank of the river
and stood watch over the entire valley.

Cord and Bird stood beside Burnett and
Hutchinson as they spoke to the other settlers,

Hendricks, Rich, McPherson, and others who stood beside their wives as they heard the news of their valley suddenly becoming what might be the scene of an Indian invasion, the likes of which they had never seen.

"So, last word was there was a band of Cheyenne Dog Soldiers comin' from up Brown's Canyon way, prob'ly came over Trout Creek Pass farther north. Anyway, they already burned a stage station and wiped out the Martin ranch. At the same time, a Comanche war party was spotted just a couple miles from here, crossing Joe's lower pasture. Both those parties are thought to number about twenty, twenty-five or so."

"Any of 'em comin' our way, John?" asked Bob Hendricks, frowning as he looked at his friend Burnett, but holding his wife close beside him.

"Not as far as we know, Bob. But who can tell which way any of 'em might go, but that ain't all."

"There's more?" asked Minerva, Burnett's wife, staring aghast at her husband.

"Well, yes an' no. There's a big bunch, the whole village I reckon, of Weenuchiu Ute under Colorow that were seen comin' from over the hill"—he pointed back up the draw of the Cochetopa toward the headwaters of the Little River—"but they have done that before and are usually peaceful, and they're headin' north like they done before, prob'ly goin' up to Golden area."

"Yeah, but there's been fights with Utes before

an' not that long ago," grumbled Nat Rich, standing close to his wife who held their one-year-old son, James, on her hip, bouncing him slightly to keep him still.

"Wal, it ain't like we went lookin' for a fight, Nat," answered Burnett.

"So, what're we gonna do?" asked Hendricks.

"Folks, this hyar is Cord Beckett, an' he's volunteered to scout the valley, see if'n he can find the different bands, maybe figger out what they might do. In the meantime, we need to get ourselves sorta forted up, you know? Joe here said he thinks if we all get together at McPherson's new store, we can all be together and fight 'em off from there, if need be."

"But that'll leave our cabins empty, they can steal ever'thin' and burn 'em down!" growled Bob Hendricks. "We can't do that!"

"Bob, you can rebuild a cabin, you can't rebuild your life. If it happens, we'll all work together to make sure ever'body comes out alright," explained Joe Hutchinson. He was the one most looked up to for leadership and he was one of the original settlers in the area. "I don't want to leave my home, it's farther away than any of yours, but I'd rather have my family safe."

———

CORD AND BIRD rode from the settlement, going north to climb the low bluffs that marked the big alluvial plain that held a few ranches and other settlers. They were traveling in the lee of the large cavalcade of Ute under Chief Colorow but kept well to the east as they moved in a somewhat parallel line, with their eyes always on the eastern edge of the valley. This was where Cord thought they would find the Comanche and probably the Cheyenne, although not too anxious to see either.

They left the mule behind, but Blue did as always and trotted out front, always scanning and scouting the trail before them. Cord and Bird rode side by side, not following any trail, but making their way through the scattered piñon, spruce and juniper that covered the plain, always doing their best to stay close to cover. They spotted the dust cloud of the village of the Ute as it moved north, hugging the foothills on the west edge of the valley, in the shadows of the Sawatch Range, but nothing showed to the east.

Cord frowned, stood in his stirrups to look to the east, glanced to Bird, "I think somethin's goin' on o'er there," pointing with his chin to the eastern edge of the mesa they now rode. He nudged Kwitcher that direction, but was a little more diligent about keeping behind cover. They were nearing the edge of the mesa, when the sounds of battle erupted with gunshots, war cries, screams, and more. Cord reined up, slipped to the ground with binoculars in one hand, his rifle in the other. He quickly tethered Kwitcher to a piñon, saw Bird doing the same, and they both moved in a crouch to the edge of the mesa, keeping a cluster of sage that hung on the edge before them. A bunch of rock hung on the edge of the mesa, overlooking the riverbed below. The battle between the Comanche and the Dog Soldiers was raging, with many of the Cheyenne taking cover in the trees, and the Comanche fighting from horseback.

Cord and Bird had bellied down at the edge, watching the fight, occasionally lifting the binoculars for a closer look, but they were less than forty yards from the scene, and maybe thirty yards above them. The Comanche made charge after charge, screaming and firing at the entrenched Cheyenne until a lull in the fight gave the Cheyenne a chance to run for their horses and swing aboard so that when the Comanche came again, many of the Dog Soldiers charged from the trees directly into the path of the Comanche and they were locked in combat, lances, tomahawks, knives were the weapons as they grappled, some tumbling from their horses, and blood flowed from wounds and bodies.

Cord and Bird were entranced with the battle until Blue began to growl and Cord looked to the dog just as he came to his feet. Cord rolled to the side, as a lance buried itself in the dirt where he had lain, but Cord grabbed the pistol from the holster as he rolled, bringing it to bear on a screaming Comanche and dropped the hammer, time and again, as the pistol bucked and spat flame, smoke, and lead. But the scream of Bird brought Cord instantly to his feet as Bird grappled with another warrior. Cord fired the pistol into the side of the attacker, causing him to jerk aside, and Bird to bring the muzzle of her rifle into the warrior's stomach and pull the trigger, blasting a hole out the man's back as he humped and fell on his face beside her.

Cord turned at the growling and snapping of Blue to see him tearing at the throat of another attacker, but Cord lifted his eyes to see another screaming warrior charging with tomahawk raised, eyes flaring, as he charged, leaping over the body of the warrior in the grip of Blue. Cord lifted his pistol, dropped the hammer, but nothing happened. He thumbed back the hammer, but the warrior was bringing the hawk down, just as Bird fired her rifle under Cord's arm, the bullet taking the charging warrior in stride, but the hawk fell on Cord's shoulder as both men stumbled and Cord fell on his back, the weight of the charging Comanche bearing him to the ground. Bird brought the barrel of her rifle down on the warrior's neck, but the Comanche was already dead, his blood and guts pouring out upon Cord, who wiggled out from under the dead body.

Cord came to his feet, noticed the sounds of the battle had subsided, and with a quick look around, he approached the edge of the bluff in a crouch and saw the remnants of the battle, with Dog Soldiers gathering their wounded and dead, stepping over the bodies of the Comanche, most of whom had already been scalped and mutilated. Cord edged back away and turned to look at Bird, "Let's get out of here. I don't know how many Comanche or Cheyenne are left, but it's not the best place for us to be. They'll be looking for these"—motioning to the four bodies of Comanche that lay at their feet, "and we don't want to be here."

They stepped aboard and started to the west and the townsfolks, but as they came from the thickets of piñon and spruce, they came face-to-face with about sixty or more Weenuchiu Ute, with the big man, Colorow sitting his mount before them. Cord reined up, but Bird kept moving toward the band, her hand held high, palm open as she greeted the chief with "*Makwa, tawigya' manakwa tüüsüwaykay. We come in peace. I am Yellow Singing Bird of the Caputa people*"—she turned slightly and motioned toward Cord—"this is my friend, Cordell Beckett."

The chief nodded, giving her permission to come near, and she moved closer, Cord beside her, "We just watched the fight between the Cheyenne Dog Soldiers and the Comanche. Many have been killed, but we go there"—nodding with her head—"to find my people. I was taken by the Comanche many summers ago, traded to the Kiowa, and now my friend brings me back to my people." She paused, "I know you are the great Colorow, leader of the Weenuchiu. It is an honor to meet you."

Colorow looked at Bird, then to Cord, and could

not help but notice the blood on both. He pointed with his chin, "You were in the fight?"

"Some came at us as we watched from the bluff. We fought back and left them where their people could find them."

"It is good." He looked at Cord again and spoke to him, "It is good what you do for this one. It is good for her to return to her people. Go in peace."

Cord was surprised that Colorow's English was very good, and he easily understood and responded with, "I am honored to meet Colorow, great chief of the Weenuchiu. May you and yours also go in peace."

32

JOURNEY

THEY DROPPED OFF THE BLUFF ON THE SOUTH SIDE OF THE long alluvial mesa, crossed the lower pasture of Hutchinson and went to the Little River, looking for a backwater pool. "I've got to get some o' this blood an' stuff off. It's dryin' out, stiffening up, and stinking!" declared Cord, looking down at the front of his shirt, vest, and trousers. He looked over at Bird who was snickering,

"You think you're the only one that has blood? Look at this!" she declared, waving a hand over her buckskin tunic.

"We'll find us a pool, jump in clothes and all, maybe get a little clean. 'Course, if you prefer, we can strip off, take a bath, wash the clothes, and put on some fresh ones."

"That's what I would prefer, but buckskin dries better when on your body," she explained, making a twisted face.

As they rode into the little settlement of Poncha Springs, they spotted Burnett coming out of the newest building that was to be a mercantile and grocery store. He waved them over and Cord stepped down as Burnett called to the others, "Beckett's back!" prompting the others to come from the store.

"So, how'd it go? What'd you find out?" queried Burnett as the others crowded around.

"Well, I don't think you need to worry about an all out attack, but I wouldn't let your guard down either. We saw the Dog Soldiers get hit by the Comanche and they had quite a fight. I reckon the Cheyenne lost maybe seven or eight, maybe more, and the Comanche lost at least half their number, prob'ly about a dozen, near as we could tell. But we kinda wore out our welcome and hightailed it outta there. But when about two hundred Ute warriors showed up with Colorow, I think both the Cheyenne and Comanche decided to pull in their horns."

Burnett frowned, "So, how many'd each band have, you know, 'fore the fight?"

"Looked to be 'bout the same, twenty, twenty-five warriors, and with the Comanche loosin' at least half their number, it'll take 'em a while to gather up their dead and leave. Same with the Cheyenne. By most standards, that's heavy losses for any war party."

"Maybe so, but that's still enough to do a lot of damage and killin'."

"But why would any of 'em come this way?

Wouldn't they just want to return to their village?" asked Minerva, Burnett's wife.

"Well, if they want to go south to Comanche country, they could go through the valley," shared Joe Hutchinson, nodding toward the pass that would take them into the San Luis Valley.

"And there's no tellin' where the Cheyenne have been camped. After Sand Creek and Julesburg, they could be just about anywhere," suggested Bob Hendricks.

"Yeah, but those are well east and north of here, so reason would say that's the general direction of their main village encampment," argued Nat Rich.

"But that still leaves the Comanche," grumbled Henry Weber.

Burnett looked at Cord, "So how far behind you might they be?"

Cord glanced to Bird, back to Burnett. "We came straight south from there, made a quick dip in the river to get rid of some blood and guts, and came here. So, I reckon it depends on how they come."

"Blood and guts? Were you wounded?"

"No, it was Comanche blood and guts," explained Cord.

Burnett looked at Joe Hutchinson, "Which way would you come, Joe?"

Hutchinson looked at Cord, "Where'd the fight take place?"

"We were at the point of the mesa, just above the

river, the fight was below us, in the trees beside the river."

"I know the place," added Hutchinson, he looked at Burnett, "If they were movin' south along the river, they would prob'ly keep goin' that way, and if they planned on goin' through the San Luis Valley, they'd come upstream on Little River, then over the pass. But dark's comin' on, I think they'd camp along the river, come up and over in the mornin'. But...they could cut across the valley and if they do that, they could get here just any time now." At that statement, the others looked to one another, turned to face the open flats below the bluff and the ridge above, as if they could see the Comanche coming at that moment.

Cord stepped forward, "That bunch of Comanche came up the river opposite the stage road. We saw 'em round about Copper Gulch, so, maybe if they came that way, they'll return that way."

Burnett looked to Hutchinson who slowly nodded his head, then back to the others, "Folks, what we know is that we don't know. So, it's up to you if you want to go back to your homes, but I think we still need to be vigilant. What say we set up a lookout schedule, put somebody up on the bluff yonder," he nodded to the hillside behind the cabins, "and let 'em keep watch and sound a warning. That way, we won't be taken by surprise, and we can mount a defense, maybe come back here at the alarm."

The others looked about, nodding and mumbling, but that idea seemed to resolve their immediate concern and the group broke up to return to their cabins. Burnett called after them, "Joe and I will make up a schedule and take it around to you!" and received mumbled responses and waves over their shoulders. Most were anxious to get back to their homes and the chores that needed done.

————

DUSK WAS SETTLING over the valley when Cord and Bird rode from the settlement, bound for Poncha Pass and ultimately the San Luis Valley. They started up the deep draw, following the course of Poncha Creek that came from the high country. As the narrow valley widened the trail, a well-used wagon trail, sided the west facing slope and rode the shoulder of the high rising hills. Within the first few miles, the road bent a little, crossed the creek, and climbed into the aspen groves, splitting the growths of white barked trees whose leaves fluttered in the cool evening breeze. The pungent smell of the aspen mixed with the tart aroma of the many pines and spruces, gave a fresh, high country smell to the foothills. Although Poncha Pass was a lesser pass compared to some others in the high country, it still rose to about 9,000 feet and crossed the foothills in the shadow of the sky scraping granite tipped mountains that were the beginning of the Sangre de Cristo range, and on the other side, the beginnings of the San Juan mountains that crawled toward the southwest corner of Colorado Territory.

Cord breathed deep of the high country air, filling his lungs with the freshness and lifted his eyes to the darkening sky where the stars were lighting their lanterns to bedeck the darkness. It was a clear night and the stars seemed to dance overhead as the tall aspen shook their leaves in the cool night air.

Bird watched Cord, smiled at his response, and asked, "Is it what you expected?"

Cord frowned, looked at the shadowy figure beside him, and asked, "Expected?"

"Of the high country. When you're in the aspen, you're in the high country."

Cord smiled, "Yeah, it's everything I expected and more." He looked around as the rising moon that was waxing full cast dim shadows and listened to the sounds of the night. Cicadas, crickets, bullfrogs in the backwater pools of the little streams, a lonesome coyote raising his anxious call to the night sky, and the shrill one-note call of the nighthawk, all blending into the harmony of the night. He smiled at Bird, "Yeah, I like it!"

Bird nudged her mare ahead on the trail as they crested the pass and the valley opened before them. From their vantage, the apex of the valley was narrow and stretched out in the shadow of the long line of sentinel peaks of the Sangre de Cristos. Cord did a double-take toward the mountains.

"That's snow!" he declared, pointing to the first peak that rose from the foothill before them.

And as he stood in his stirrups, he was amazed at the beauty of the moonlit mountains and the valley that lay below, marked with the shadow of the long San Luis Creek that came from near where they sat. To his right, foothills and mesas rose from the valley floor and stretched into the west and the beginnings of the San Juan mountains.

Cord smiled broadly, "It feels like I'm home!" he whispered.

Bird whispered, "This is my home."

She nudged her mount to the right side of the valley, along the grassy flats of a low-rising mesa that was dotted with aspen groves and whose shoulders were thick with the white barked beauties. She led them into the aspen, spotted a suitable clearing and reined up, stepped down, looked to Cord as he also stepped down, and pointed to the edge of the trees, "There's water there, let the animals drink, then we'll roll out the blankets and sleep."

Cord chuckled, looked at her, "So, since this is your home that makes you the boss?"

Bird smiled, nodded, and began to gather some firewood as Cord led the animals away.

33

HOT SPRINGS

THEY WERE MEMORIES SHE HAD HARBORED FOR EIGHT years, the memories of a ten-year-old girl that had been stolen from her people, her family, her home, and her only connection to her family was the memories of her childhood. Memories that included the land where her people lived and traveled, for her people were a migrating tribe of Caputa Ute, but this land had been their home, even though that home was a hide lodge carried on a travois as they followed the herds of buffalo, the ripening of berries and other plants used for their foods and medicines, and the always changing seasons.

Now they rode south, paralleling the San Luis creek that meandered in the bottom of the great San Luis Valley that lay in the shadows of the Sangre de Cristo mountains, and above the San Juan Mountain range. This expansive valley lay like a pale green, buff colored blanket across the land, pocked with yucca, cacti, buffalo grass and random bunches of sage, grease wood and rabbit brush. There was nothing to hinder the view from where they rode on the shoulders of the foothills on the west edge of the valley for they were above the valley floor, riding near the tree line of the deep green junipers and piñon.

Bird was in the lead and would often rein up, looking around, searching for anything familiar. She stood in her stirrups and shaded her eyes from the low rising sun that was slowly peeking over the Sangres, bending bright rays to illuminate the wide valley. There were no shadows for there was nothing standing tall enough to cast a shadow, save the horses they rode. Cord leaned on the pommel of his saddle, listening to the almost silent whispering whistle of the breeze that stirred the buffalo grass like the low waves of a lake, and smelling the pungent juniper, and the dusky scent of the sage. But what captured his attention, was the amazing sight of the mountains of the Sangre de Cristo range that marched unhindered to the south, showing clefts with snow that accented the steep mountainsides that were nothing but shale and granite. The grey peak tips seemed to scratch the blue of the cloudless sky, and the almost black blankets that lay on their shoulders faded into the dusky colors of the valley bottom, while the San Luis creek robed itself in the greens of willows, cottonwoods, chokecherry, service berry, and kinnikinnick, as it wandered ever southward.

She turned to look at Cord, a broad smile splitting her face as she appeared to bounce in her saddle,
her excitement contagious, "Yes! I remember! This is
the valley my people would sometimes make their
summer camp, near the hot springs! We would pitch
our lodges near the trees, or up in that valley with
the little creek!" She twisted around in her saddle to
point to the creek coming from the cut in the hills on
the west edge of the valley, still a few miles from
where they sat. "We are close, I can feel it!" she
declared as she dug heels to the ribs of her mount
and took off at a canter.

Cord grinned, watched her mare kicking up some
dust and nudged Kwitcher to follow, choosing to
keep the stallion to a brisk walk, his long legs
stretching out and his mouth tugging at the reins as
he stretched out his nose to the dust of the white
mare. He wanted to run, but Cord held him back, the
mule behind him plodding along and Blue beside
him as they watched the eager Bird leaving a trail of
dust.

Finger ridges of the timber covered hills
stretched out into the valley like the long tentacles of
some ocean monster that Cord had read about in the
adventures of the sea going buccaneers that he
enjoyed as a youth. He chuckled at his memory but
nodded to himself at the thought of octopus limbs as
mountain ridges. Bird finally stopped, twisted
around in her saddle to give Cord an exasperated

look, wondering why he was so slow, but she smiled as he came alongside.

The first few miles after they left camp in the early morning, moved over the many ridges and they were always up and down, but the wide flanks of the foothills stretched out and lay like a blanket of sage and buffalo grass that slowly sloped into the valley bottom. They kept near the trees, always cautious and determined to have cover near as this wide valley seemed to swallow them and their expectations as it stretched out so many miles in every direction, even though Cord could not get enough of the view of the mountains. They had come about twelve to thirteen miles when the long slope dropped into a narrow valley that carried a meandering creek and all the greenery with it. It was an enticing sight and they let the horses take their own pace as they smelled the water and the grasses. When they pulled up at creek's edge, Cord stood in his stirrups and looked up the valley that seemed to cut its way through the foothills from the higher San Juan mountains.

They stepped down, let the horses and mule graze in the deep grass as they munched on a couple handfuls of jerky, enjoying the cool of the day and using the cups to scoop up some cold water from the creek. Before them stood a solitary cone shaped hill, freckled with scrub piñon and buckbrush, and Cord nodded, looked to Bird, "What say we climb that, have a look around?"

Bird nodded, knowing the animals would not stray from the grass and water, their reins and lead rope trailing that kept them ground tied, and she stood to go with Cord.

When they neared the crest of the cone, scattered rocks offered handholds and steps to make the last few feet easier, and once on the crest, Cord bellied down, keeping from skylining himself, and lifted the binoculars and began his scan. Bird lay beside him, looking at the valley from their higher vantage point. Cord said, "Well, there's some antelope out yonder, some horses down there"—pointing to a spot that appeared to have a wispy cloud above it—"but not much else, anywhere."

He handed the binoculars to Bird, sat up and watched her as she slowly scanned the land before them. He saw her pause as she looked to the south where he had seen some horses and waited for her reaction. She dropped the glasses, rolled to her side to look at Cord, "That's the hot springs! Those horses could be my people!"

Cord chuckled, "Maybe, but don't get in a big hurry. We don't know who they are and if they're friendly or not!"

But they were not Bird's people. As they neared, Cord and Bird saw the horses were a team of four horses in harness, but grazing on the nearby grass, while the wagon sat near the springs and some people were in the water, enjoying the hot springs. When Cord called out, "Hello the camp!"

They heard a squeal, a shout, and a voice called, "Stay where you are!" followed by considerable splashing about. Cord frowned, leaned forward on his pommel, and spotted two or three figures, all clad in women's underclothes, soaking wet, climbing from the water, and hustling to the back of the wagon. Cord looked at Bird, back at the ruckus, "I think they're all women!" he declared, disbelieving what he had seen. He was certain it was at least three women, each clad in chemise and pantaloons, that scampered from the water. As he looked into the steamy mist, a fully clad figure emerged, a rifle in hand and growling, "What'chu want?"

It was definitely a woman's voice, although considerably gruff, and he shook his head, "We thought you might be some people we knew but reckon not. Didn't see your wagon till we was up close. Don't mean no harm, we'll just keep on movin'."

"Hold it! Don'tchu go anywhere." As she spoke, two others came to her side, also clothed and holding rifles at the ready. The speaker said as she motioned with the barrel of her rifle, "She your woman?"

"She's my friend. Her name is Yellow Singing Bird, I'm Cordell Beckett. Say, ain'tchu got any men with you?"

"Ain't none o' yore bizness!" growled the woman, moving her rifle as if to wave their visitors away.

"Ma'am, we mean you no harm. We're looking to

find the village of the Caputa Ute, Bird's people. She was stolen from 'em a few years back and wants to get back to her family. Have you folks seen anything that might be a village, you know, teepees an' such, it'd be a good-sized village, I reckon."

"Ain't seen any injuns since them Apache hit our wagons."

Cord frowned, stood in his stirrups to try to see through the rising cloud of steam, "Are you all there is?"

"Go on! Scram 'fore I shoot you!" growled the woman, but one of the others pleaded,

"Wait a minute Gert, they might help us." The second woman stepped forward, the muzzle of her rifle pointed down to the ground as she looked from Bird to Cord, "I'm Adelaide, the other'n over there is Blanche"—and with a nod toward the first woman— "and she's Gertrude, Gert for short."

"Pleased to meet you ladies, now how might we help you?"

"We don't know where we are or how to get anywhere there might be people. Can you help us?"

Cord nodded to Bird, and both stepped down, and Cord said, "Well, you're going in the right direction. This bit of a trail you're on is part of the Old Spanish Trail, and it'll take you up through that cut" —he began as he turned to point to the north at the valley's mouth—"and over a bit of a pass. You can make it fine with your wagon, and it'll take you down the other side and at the bottom is a little settlement called Poncha Springs. We left there yesterday, and there's several families, good folks. I'm sure you'll be welcome there."

The women looked at one another, relief showing on their faces. Gert then stepped forward and asked, "Could you guide us there, mister?"

Cord chuckled, "You don't need a guide. You just need to try to stay near cover, keep your eyes open and weapons handy, you know, like you have been." Cord chuckled, glanced to Bird, back to the women, "You can be there by late tomorrow."

"You hear that, girls? Tomorrow!" said Gert, and she turned back, "Say, either of you know anything 'bout tendin' wounds? We got a couple our men in the wagon, they ain't doin' so well after takin' some arrows from the Apache a couple days back."

Cord looked to Bird who nodded and motioned to Adelaide to take her to the wagon, and she followed the woman to the back tailgate. As they climbed in, Bird could smell the stench of festering wounds, and lifted the canvas of the wagon for more light. She made a quick scan of both men, who were semi-conscious and moaning, then turned to the back of the wagon, looked at the women and said, "Adelaide, get a shovel and dig some yucca root," she pointed out the spiny yucca, then turned to the other woman, "Blanche, would you gather a couple hand-fuls of sage leaves, the soft ones? And then get some big prickly pear pads, five or six." And pointed those out to the woman. "Gert, you come help me," stated

Bird, as she stepped aside for the woman. Bird smiled at Cord, "Start a fire so we can burn off the spines from the prickly pear." Cord grinned, nodded and looked around for any wood, finding only the dried pieces of cholla and sage, but gathering an armful and laying out a fire.

Bird turned back to the men. When Gert stepped in, she said, "Strip away their clothes from the wounds, wipe them off, then we'll wash them."

"We tried washin' 'em, but we ain't got no soap," grumbled Gert.

Bird smiled, "That's what the yucca root is for, soap."

"Oh!" said Gert and set to work.

It took a good two hours to finish dressing the wounds of the men. With poultices made from Bear Root that Bird had in her kit, and sage leaves, and using the prickly pear pads after peeling off the skin on one side, as a wound cover over the poultice, then binding the wounds with clean strips of cloth from the wagon, the men were in much better shape and the women were more optimistic than before.

Cord and Bird bid the women goodbye and resumed their trek southward, but the sun was high over their right shoulders and there was not a lot of daylight left in the day, but they were optimistic as to their journey's end.

34

VILLAGE

Dusk was embracing the hillsides and coloring the valleys with darkness as they turned to the west to move up the banks of the Saguache Creek, but in the distance, the glow of cookfires danced among the treetops. When the lights were seen, Bird turned to look at Cord, anticipation dancing in her eyes and nervousness showing in her movements. She nudged the mare close to Kwitcher and said, "We cannot go into the village unseen. We must make our presence known."

"What do you suggest? What do you want me to do, whistle, shout, shoot my gun, what?" he chuckled, shaking his head.

She slapped his shoulder, laughing, "You know what I mean, we can be talking, slapping leather, anything so they know we are not sneaking up on them."

Cord nodded, started whistling and laughing,

slapped his reins on his canvas britches, and they moved toward the lights. The horses had heads lifted, ears pricked, as they stepped out, the mule plodded behind and Blue moved beside Kwitcher. As they approached, three warriors came from the shadows to stand before them, rifles in hand to stop them. "*Tutüskwa!*"

Bird spoke, "*Makwa. Mönöni tünakwa tüüsüwaykay.* We come in peace. I am Yellow Singing Bird of the Caputa Ute, this is my friend, Cordell Beckett. *Nüga'panaakay nuuwaga.* I return to my people."

The men stood in silence, looking from Bird to Cord by the dim light of the cookfires and the shadows of dusk. One stepped forward, "Get down, we will take you into the camp."

Cord and Bird stepped down, Cord motioned Blue to his side, and they walked together behind the three men as they entered the encampment, walking between the hide lodges, making their way to the central area circle that held several cookfires with women busy at work preparing their meals. As they moved further into the encampment, Cord noticed the odor of drying hides stretched on racks, jerky curing over smoking coals, hair with bear grease that gave it a sheen in the dim light, dust from the many feet moving the dirt as they walked or came near to stare, everywhere there was life, people moving, children playing, babies fussing, dogs barking, and more. Cord realized that he was a touch nervous, concerned, and had his hand resting on the butt of his pistol under his duster, but he did his best to appear casual, friendly, unthreatening. All about him, stoic warriors stood, women forming the second rank, all staring as the strangers entered their presence.

They were brought before a stately looking man with a blanket about his shoulders, but his beaded tunic, hair pipe bone necklace, and beaded and fringed leggings over beaded moccasins told of a prominent leader. His wrinkled face showed no emotion as he glared at Cord and Bird and addressed himself to Bird.

"Why do you come into our village, uninvited?"

"Is it the great Chief Ouray that we stand before?" queried Bird, standing tall and unintimidated before the great chief.

"I am Ouray," and with a slight nod to his side, "my woman is Chipeta."

"I am Yellow Singing Bird, my father is White Eagle, my mother is Bird that Walks on Water. The Caputa are my people. I was taken from this village many years ago when the Comanche raided and killed many and stole others. I was traded to the Kiowa, and now I come back to my people with my friend, Cordell Beckett."

There was a stirring among the people as many heard the words of Bird, and a bit of a commotion rose behind them as the group moved about and one pushed her way close. She stood beside the visitors, frowning, and interrupted, "I am Night Wind, Yellow Singing Bird is my sister!" She moved beside Bird and the two women embraced, tears readily flowing.

Ouray watched, waited until the women separated, and said, "You are welcome to your homeland and people. Those you spoke of have crossed over, Night Wind and her family are here." He looked to Night Wind, "Take these to your lodge, we will talk more after the sun shows again."

Night Wind nodded, took Bird's hand and with a nod to Cord, they turned and started through the village to go to Night Wind's lodge. Cord dropped his hand to Blue's head, stroked his scruff and with reins and lead rope in hand, he led the horses and mule and followed the women. Near the edge of the village, Night Wind stopped, called to her man, Broken Arrow, who came from the lodge, frowning as he looked at the visitors before him. Night Wind quickly explained, Arrow nodded and returned into the lodge without speaking or even acknowledging the visitors and Night Wind motioned for them to be seated on a blanket and before a willow backrest.

As the women chattered, Cord looked about, feeling very out-of-place and when Bird looked his way, he interjected, "I think I'll go yonder, into the trees, find us a camp and make ready for the night. You stay here with Night Wind, enjoy your time." He stood, smiled at Bird, turned, and went to the trees.

The village lay in a bit of a bowl, with rimrock ridges and buttes rising on three sides and the valley floor open below. A small spring-fed creek came from the hills, cutting through the trees near Cord's camp, offering ample water for the horses, mule, and them. Cord had stretched out his blankets near the trees, the gear stacked under a bigger juniper, and Cord's blankets under the wider spanning branches of a mature ponderosa.

It was before first light when he came from his blankets, stood, stretched, and looked about. Things were always different in the light of day, even the dim light of pre-dawn morning, and he chuckled as he looked around at his lonesome camp. Apparently Bird had stayed with her sister, and rightly so, but still he missed her. There had been a lot of things going through his mind after he left the village and made his camp. With the reunion of Bird and her sister, the news of the loss of her parents, and the welcoming of the band, his mind was a jumble of thoughts, regrets, and recriminations. He glanced to his saddlebags, saw the corner of the old Bible, and let a slow grin split his face. With a glance Heaven-ward, he bent down, pulled out the Bible and strapped on his belt and pistol, hung the binoculars around his neck, slipped on his duster and hat, grabbed his rifle, and started for the ridge above his camp.

He found a good promontory and he looked at the land that lay to the east in the shadows of the Sangre de Cristo and watched as the slow rising sun began to stretch the shadows of the mountains across the wide valley pockmarked with sage and cacti. He sat down on a flat rock, leaned the rifle beside him and opened the Bible. His father had always favored the book of Ecclesiastes and he flipped the pages until he came to a well-marked chapter and settled on chapter ten, verse ten, *What-soever thy hand findeth to do, do it with thy might; for there is no work, nor device, nor knowledge, nor wisdom in the grave, whither thou goest.* Cord chuckled, remembering the times his father had quoted the first of that verse about working with thy might. That was his admonition to Cord to *"always do your best job, no matter what you're doing, always do your best."* Cord grinned at the remembrance, glanced at the page and his eyes settled on the verse just before that, verse 9 *Live joyfully with the wife whom thou lovest all the days of the life of thy vanity, which he hath given thee under the sun...for that is thy portion in this life...*

His mind immediately went to Bird, seeing her smiling face before him, hearing her laughter, watching her move. He had thought about her in that way before, but those thoughts were probably far from her mind now, this was a time of remembrance and renewal for her, not him.

Cord looked to Heaven, *So Lord, whatsoever thy hand findeth to do...does that mean I'm on the right track, goin' after those outlaws that killed my family? Is that what I'm supposed to do? What about forgiveness?* He paused, looking about, remembering their time at the fort and the meeting with the preacher there, his thoughts of forgiveness and more. But what about justice? Those men are still going wild, killing, stealing, destroying. Isn't it the right thing to do to bring them to justice? *Is that what I'm supposed to do—do it with all thy might?*

He breathed heavily, shook his head, and looked around as the rising sun lifted the curtain on another day and revealed all the beauty of the wide valley and the distant mountains before him, *Lord, you sure did a fine job with those mountains. You musta done that with all your might.* As he watched the golden orb slowly begin to launch lances of golden white across the valley to stretch to the mountains behind him, Cord just stared in wonder and awe, reveling in the majesty of the Creator.

He bowed his head, said a simple prayer for guidance and protection and wisdom for the day and the way, asked for blessings on Bird and her family, and with a simple Amen, rose and started back to his camp. He fixed himself a pot of coffee, tossed some leftover biscuits into the frying pan with the bacon and had himself a bit of breakfast. He chuckled, began packing things together, and was soon ready to leave. With another look about, he stepped aboard, grabbed the lead of the mule, the rein of Bird's mare and started back to the lodge of Night Wind. No one was moving around the lodge and Cord stepped down, tethered the mare nearby, swung back aboard and quietly rode around the camp and took to the trail north.

His plan was to take the trail over Poncha Pass, drop into the Arkansas valley and go north to Chalk Creek, then on to Oro City, and if he found some of the Red Legs he would decide what he would do then, but he was leaning a little more to vengeance or justice, than he was to forgiveness. But that was another day, this day was for traveling.

————

ALWAYS WANTING to see something new, Cord crossed the valley bottom and took to the trees that were the edge of the black timber on the flanks of the Sangre de Cristo mountains. He loved the smell of the pines and spruce, the look of the towering ponderosa, the thick growing lodgepole pine, and the creatures of the mountainous forests. But when he smelled a less than pleasant odor and the horses grew skittish, Blue began to growl, he thought he might be in trouble. He stepped down, grabbed the Sharps from the pack mule, checked the load and began to walk along the bit of game trail they followed, watching and always with that dank stink in the air, but when the timber trembled and the mountain seemed to move with the roar that rattled his senses, he froze in place, looking fearfully about. The sudden snap and crashing that came from the trees warned of trouble coming.

Cord bent, twisted about, searching for whatever was making the noise, and when he dropped to one knee to look below the wide stretching branches of a massive spruce, he saw a wall of dark brown that seemed to be rolling down the mountainside, but it was a monstrous Grizzly, his mouth gaping, showing the pink of his mouth, the snapping of his jaws and the roar as slobbers flew to the side as he slashed the air with his muzzle, slapping at nothing and everything with his huge paws that showed claws longer than Cord's fingers.

Suddenly the big bruin stopped, slapped at the air before him, let out a roar that made the trees tremble, and rose to his hind legs, jaws snapping, slobbers flying, and the roar rattling even the limbs of the trees about him. When he rose up, he stood what appeared to be between nine and ten feet tall, his belly and chest showing silver tipped hair, but his head swiveled side to side as if he had not seen anything threatening, although Cord and the horse, mule and Blue were less than thirty feet away. Cord froze in place, Blue beside him was growling and trembling, and the big stallion lowered his head, moving it slowly, as his legs trembled. The mule had his head lifted, ears forward, and eyes glaring at the threat before him looking as if he was ready to go to battle. But the bear quieted, dropped to all fours, and with one look over his shoulder, ambled off into the thicker timber.

"It was good you did not shoot," came a soft voice from behind him. A voice that startled Cord almost as much as the grizzly, but he turned to see

Bird, standing with her rifle in hand and smiling. "You left, why?"

Cord rose, stroked Blue behind the ears to settle him, stepped beside Kwitcher to touch and calm him, all while looking at Bird. "I thought you wanted to stay with your family. They are your people, isn't that why we came all this way?"

"Yes, but you are also my family. I will go with you," she smiled, stepping closer.

A LOOK AT BOOK TWO:
TINCUP

DEVASTATION. VENGEANCE. WILD WEST ACTION.

Still reeling from the aftermath of a brutal attack that shattered his family and razed his home to ashes, Cordell Beckett emerges from the wreckage transformed. It took three years to make a man out of a boy, but that man has begun his chase and now finds himself in the gold fields of the Wild West.

With his loyal dog by his side and the vast expanse of the frontier stretching out before him, Cordell casts a long shadow over the trail, his presence striking fear into the hearts of outlaws. Yet, as he draws closer to his quarry, doubt gnaws at him. Will he succeed in his quest for vengeance...or will he falter at the threshold of his life's purpose?

In a landscape teeming with danger and opportunity, join along on Cordell's journey as his quest for retribution leads him down a path fraught with the unknown. Buy your copy of this classic Western today!

AVAILABLE JULY 2024

ABOUT THE AUTHOR

Born and raised in Colorado into a family of ranchers and cowboys, B.N. Rundell is the youngest of seven sons. Juggling bull riding, skiing, and high school, graduation was a launching pad for a hitch in the Army Paratroopers. After the army, he finished his college education in Springfield, MO, and together with his wife and growing family, entered the ministry as a Baptist preacher.

With many years as a successful pastor and educator, he retired from the ministry and followed in the footsteps of his entrepreneurial father and started a successful insurance agency, which is now in the hands of his trusted nephew. Having finally realized his life-long dream, B.N. has turned his efforts to writing a variety of books, from children's picture books and young adult adventure books, to the historical fiction and Western genres, which are his first loves.

NOTES

11. Visitors

1. *Charles Curtis became the 31st Vice President of the U.S.*